lucky stars

ALSO BY LUCY FRANK
The Annoyance Bureau
Just Ask Iris
Oy, Joy!
Will You Be My Brussels Sprout?
I Am an Artichoke

lucky
stars

lucy frank

Aladdin Paperbacks
NEW YORK LONDON TORONTO SYDNEY

This book is a work of fiction. Any references to historical events, real people, or real locales are used fictitiously. Other names, characters, places, and incidents are the product of the author's imagination, and any resemblance to actual events or locales or persons, living or dead, is entirely coincidental.

ALADDIN PAPERBACKS
An imprint of Simon & Schuster Children's Publishing Division
1230 Avenue of the Americas, New York, NY 10020
Copyright © 2005 by Lucy Frank
All rights reserved, including the right of reproduction in whole
or in part in any form.
ALADDIN PAPERBACKS and colophon are trademarks of
Simon & Schuster, Inc.
Also available in an Atheneum Books for Young Readers hardcover edition.
Designed by name Kristin Smith
The text of this book was set in Scherzo.
Manufactured in the United States of America
First Aladdin Paperbacks edition November 2006
10 9 8 7 6 5 4 3 2 1
The Library of Congress has cataloged the hardcover edition as follows:
Frank, Lucy.
Lucky stars / Lucy Frank.—1st ed.
p.   cm.
"A Richard Jackson Book."
Summary: Music entwines Kira, a thirteen-year-old singer, who hates that her
father makes her perform for money on New York City subway platforms;
Eugene, the class clown; and Jake, who longs to sing and to approach Kira,
but feels held back by his stuttering.
ISBN-13: 978-0-689-85933-5 (hc.)
ISBN-10: 0-689-85933-3 (hc.)
ISBN-13: 978-0-689-85934-2 (pbk.)
ISBN-10: 0-689-85934-1 (pbk.)

For Peter, whose love of music
has so deepened mine

contents

"How Can I Tell Grandma?"

Grandma was wrong. Dad's there, right where he said he'd be on the platform when I step off the train. "Look at you! All cute and grown-up!" he says. "Guys!" he tells my little half brothers. "Say hello to your big sister! Ki, I got you something!"

Before my emergency contact card is back in my pocket, he reaches into the bag on Charlie's stroller and pulls out a long, fluffy, feathered scarf. The feathers are crazy county-fair colors: peacock blue, acid green, yellow, purple, hot pink. He winds it around my neck. It's soft and tickly against my chin.

Grandma warned me not to expect a present from him. She was wrong about that, too. I throw my arms around him. "It's great, Dad! I love it."

He holds me at arm's length and looks me over. "I don't know," he says, checking out the jacket Aunt Phyllis got me for Christmas. He's wearing his same leather jacket. He's got his same ponytail and his cowboy boots. "It don't exactly go with that lavender."

"It's not lavender, Dad," I inform him. "It's peri- winkle. With vapor gray." That sounded so cool when Aunt Phyllis read it to me from the catalog. I can't believe how lame it sounds now. At least I ditched the snow boots. The first thing I did, the second the train pulled out, was take off the giant clumpers and shove them under the seat. Where they remain. I'm probably fooling myself that they'll still be there waiting when I go back to Claryville. But, hey, Dad was here waiting, and I've got four days till I have to worry about it.

"I like your beard, Dad," I tell him. "The boys are huge!"

"You hear that, guys?" Dad pulls Chris's thumb out of his mouth, then leans down and lifts Charlie's cap up off his eyes. "Come on, Chazman! Give Ki a smile. Tell her all the things we're gonna do. None of that corny tourist stuff, Ki. I told them, we're gonna show you the real New York music scene. From the inside. Right, guys?"

Charlie pulls the cap over his face again. Chris looks at me like I might bite.

"What, you've forgotten how to smile?" Dad says. "You remember Kira!"

"It's fine," I say. The boys haven't seen me since Dad brought them up to Grandma's last summer.

That's a long time when you're three and five. "You don't have to smile if you don't want," I tell them.

Dad folds the stroller and picks up Charlie so we can get on the escalator. Once we're at the top he grabs my bags and hangs them on the stroller. I refused to take the flowered suitcase. My clothes are rolled up in my backpack. But I have two shopping bags filled with other stuff Grandma's bought them at various times and then was too pissed to send, plus a gigantic bag of Christmas candy. All the diabetics and people with, like, denture problems at Pine Manor, where she works, gave us theirs.

"You hungry, Ki? You need something to eat?" Dad shouts as we start walking. You have to shout to be heard in here. Penn Station is echoey and blarey. And huge. It's mind-boggling how many people there are milling around. And so many stores and stands and kiosks. All of which are smelling good to me. I did really well staying out of the Pine Manor chocolates on the train. Just breathing this burger-y-doughnut-y air makes my stomach growl.

"I'm starved!" I shout back.

"Excellent! You ever had real New York pizza?" he says.

"How would I have had real New York pizza,

Dad? I've only been here once, remember?" Five years ago. "And you were too busy marrying Tammy to get me any."

"Well, we'll have to rectify that, won't we, guys!" he tells the boys.

First, though, we stop at a pay phone. I use the pocketful of change Grandma gave me to call her at work and tell her about the scarf, and that the train ride down the Hudson was as gorgeous as everyone has said, and that Dad and the boys look great.

"Well," Grandma says. "I'm glad to hear it! Did he give you the money for your ticket?"

"Grandma, I just got here."

She's having a hard time forgiving him for not calling on Christmas day. And for waiting to invite me till the day after. Also for asking me if I'm still short enough to get by with a half-fare ticket. I haven't been twelve in three months. I knew he was just yanking her chain, but I should never have told her about it.

"Did you tell Russell that if he disappoints you or lets you down or upsets you in any way, I will personally come down and clean his clock?" she says now.

"No, I didn't!" I tell her. "It's fine, Grandma. Really. Everything's gonna be fine."

"Yeah, well, just make sure your baloney detectors are working," she says. Grandma swears she can smell baloney a hundred miles off, which just happens to be the distance between Claryville and New York City.

"She said to give the boys a big kiss and say hi to Tammy," I tell Dad when I get off the phone. That's another thing Grandma's upset about—that Tammy always has another reason why she can't come up to visit. And that she didn't call to say how they liked their presents. "I mean, I know he was out on tour," Grandma said. "But that don't excuse Tammy."

"So, how've you been spending your vacation?" Dad asks as we walk through the station. "What's new up there in boony land? You still knocking 'em dead over at the old folks' home?"

"I guess." I hate it when he calls Claryville boony land. But I already told him on the phone yesterday that Aunt Phyllis hired me to sing at her office party this year. And that I sang "O Holy Night" at the Christmas Eve service. "I'm still singing at the Pine Manor Sunday socials, if that's what you mean. And I'm performing at their New Year's Eve party."

Dad laughs. "You and old man Corrigan?" Dad knows Mr. Corrigan. He's a resident at Pine Manor now, but he used to play piano in the bars and clubs around town. "Should auld acquaintance be forgot," he sings in a quavery voice.

"He doesn't sound like that, Dad!" Mr. Corrigan may be eighty-four, but he's my friend. I love Mr. Corrigan. "He's still really sharp. And I'm the one who sings."

Dad shakes his head. "Oh, man! I called right in the nick of time, didn't I? Kira, you are in serious need of a life!"

I see his point. So when he says, "What else is doing?" I say, "Other than that, hmmm, let's see. There's beetle patrol." He turns to me blankly. "You know, those little spotted ladybugs that look so cute and smell so bad? The ones that come in through the walls every winter and buzz around everywhere and fry themselves on the woodstove? I vacuumed up two hundred thirty-three yesterday. I counted. And one flew into Grandma's coffee. And this morning one landed in her Raisin Bran, and she didn't have her glasses on."

I've got his attention now.

"And she swallowed it?"

"You mean them?" I nod.

"Uh-oh. Did she blow a gasket?"

"Oh, yeah." I'd punch anyone else making fun of

Grandma. She's raised me since I was five. But it feels good to make him laugh. "Oh, yeah!" I say again. "We've got so many ladybugs I've started naming them. "There's Spot, Spotty, Speckles, Spotless . . . Dot—"

"Whoa, there!" Dad holds up a hand. "Watch your step, Ki!" Dot's Grandma's name.

"You asked what I was doing. What about you, Dad?"

On the phone last night my two friends couldn't stop talking about Dad's band, asking if I'd sing with him if he invited me, since he did invite me to sing at his wedding, when I was, like, eight. Asking what I'd wear. Saying stuff like, "One day, Pine Manor, the next, the stars."

"Dad, so how's the band?"

"Actually," he says. "To tell you the truth, the band's taking a little breather at the moment. Which is why I thought this was the perfect time to get you down. Hey!" he tells Chris. "I see a pizza place over there. Let's go get Ki some pizza."

"You think they have a bathroom?" I ask as we step up to the counter.

"I doubt it." Dad takes his wallet from his jeans pocket, peers inside, checks the price list on the wall, snorts, and puts his wallet back into his pocket.

"Them slices don't look as good as I was hoping," he says. "We'll keep going."

They looked pretty good to me, but we walk on, out of the main train station now, into a long, tiled hallway with a curved-tile ceiling. It's like walking in an endless tube. Dad explains about MetroCards, subway lines, uptown, downtown, locals, expresses. I'm too busy trying to look at everything to get it all.

Fitting two little boys, my bags, and the stroller through the turnstiles is a challenge, but we manage that and the stairs. The subway platform's as packed as the station. The noise level's crazy. So many people push onto the train it's a miracle anyone can get out.

I'm not scared, though. I hold tightly to Dad's arm when he wheels Charlie onto the train, but I don't think Grandma's right about the subway being full of muggers and pickpockets. I see people reading newspapers, listening to music, eating McDonald's. I see a woman reading the Bible, another fixing her eyeshadow, three girls my age flirting with some boys across the aisle. What I don't see is anyone over the age of three in a periwinkle jacket. I'm so glad I ditched the snow boots.

"Chris, hold on to Kira," Dad says when we get off. "Ki, do me a favor. Grab the front of the stroller so we can go up the steps. We're gonna take a little tour now. Ki, you're about to see the stars of tomorrow."

He leads us down another corridor. This one is grimier. It smells like dirt. "What are these nasty black blobs on the floor?" I ask Dad.

"Fifty years worth of chewing gum," he says. "Possibly a hundred. But what are you looking at the ground for?" He nods toward a niche at the top of the stairs where a guy with gray dreadlocks is playing the flute. He's playing jazz.

"Wow. What's he doing down here?" I say. "He's really good!"

Dad grins at me. "This is what I'm saying! Welcome to New York, Ki! You want to meet him?" He wheels the stroller over. "Yo, man, whassup?"

The guy stops playing. "Hey, Russ, what's happening?" he says as he and Dad go through a whole complicated handshake. "Whassup, big man?" he says to Chris. "How you doin', Shorty?" he asks Charlie.

"I'm not Shorty," Charlie tells him. It's the first thing I've heard either boy say.

"Meet my daughter," Dad says. "Kira, say hello to Malik."

I try not to stare at Malik's beard, which has a little skinny braid in the middle of it. The braid has a blue and white bead on the end. "Hey," I say.

"Kira's a singer," Dad says as Malik shakes my hand. "This here's the little girl with the big pipes. Kira can sing anything."

"Not really," I tell him.

"Don't listen to her," Dad says. "So, how's business? Where're all your tapes and CDs today?"

"Sold 'em." Malik smiles at me. "I like that feather boa, young lady. Thank you, baby," he tells a girl who's tossed a dollar in his flute case, which is filled with bills and change. Then he goes back to playing.

"How do you know him?" I ask Dad as we keep walking.

He laughs. "It's a small world, this music world. Malik does real well down here. Picks up some gigs from it too. Club dates, parties . . ." He nods toward an old man in filthy pants and broken-down shoes sitting on the floor with a sign next to him: PLEASE HELP ME GET SOMETHING TO EAT. I GOT HIT ON THE HEAD. I SUFFER FROM BLACKOUTS. The man has no socks and no coat. I think about giving him some money, but all I have is the twenty-dollar bill Grandma's pinned to the inside of my shirt. "It used to be mostly guys like that down here," Dad says. "Now, everywhere you turn there's music. It's a whole underground world of music."

At the next set of stairs I pick up the front of the

stroller before he asks. I'm hearing more music now. A hip-hop beat. The thump of a drum track. There's a big circle of people, clapping and whistling. We have to say "Excuse me, excuse me!" to get close enough to see. It's break dancers—four skinny boys in tank tops and big jeans and do-rags. One of them, who I doubt is any older than me, is walking on his hands. Charlie is starting to get fussy, but we watch them for a long time.

"Amazing, huh?" Dad says. "I see them here a lot." He nods toward two girls stepping up to drop money in their box. "They rake it in, too."

More stairs, more tunnels, another train, more music: an old man this time, doing a crazy tap-dance thing, clacking two spoons together, tapping them on his arms, his legs, his cheeks, his nose. No more places to eat, though, and no bathrooms. At the other end of that station, or maybe it's another station, a man dances with a doll as tall as he is, with long, black curly hair and a short, ruffly skirt. Her high heels are glued to his shoes and his hands are in her pockets, so that when his hips move, hers wiggle too. "She's hot, right?" Dad says as the man tilts her backward, dips her, swings her around. People keep stepping up and tossing money in his box. Some people speaking a foreign language are videotaping him. Everyone except Chris and Charlie is smiling and laughing. Dad hands Charlie a pacifier, and says something in Spanish to the man. He answers, calling Dad "Russell."

"How do you know all these guys?" I ask Dad. "I didn't know you spoke Spanish."

"*Sí, mi amor!* There's a lot of things you don't know about me," he says, grinning. "Welcome to New York, Ki. You ready to check out one more station? We can shoot across to Grand Central. There's always really cool acts over there."

"Sure!" I say, even though my stomach's growling nonstop now. And if I'm dying for a bathroom, I know the boys must be.

By the time we come out, we've seen a man singing "La Bamba" in the middle of the platform, a man playing a violin that looks like it's made of glass, a man drumming on a bunch of upside-down plastic buckets. Dad would have kept going, but Chris and Charlie have totally had it. It's almost dark. My backpack feels like it's filled with cement.

"I hope you're not expecting, like, Trump Tower," he says as we turn off a big, wide, busy street onto a smaller one.

"Long as it has a bathroom," I tell him.

It's not as big as the building he lived in the last

time we were down, but that could be because I was so much smaller. It's brick, with fire escapes on the front, and a wide flight of stairs leading up to a big, carved wooden door.

He doesn't go up those stairs, though. After he unbuckles Charlie and folds the stroller, he takes out a bunch of keys and unlocks the padlock on the gate that's part of this fence enclosing a flight of metal steps.

I follow him down the steps to a narrow paved area under the building stairs.

It's like going down into a cave. A cave filled with trash barrels.

He flips on another light and unlocks another iron gate. We step into a little entryway. There are no garbage cans in here. But there's a rusty bird-cage, a pile of flowerpots, a squashed-in shopping cart, and an old ironing board. It doesn't smell like garbage, but it smells a lot like the subway.

"This is where you live?" I ask as he unlocks the door. I don't know what I was expecting. Not Trump Tower. But not this, either.

My heart sinks even more when I see inside.

One thing: I'll be safe down here. No one can break in. But how can I tell Grandma?

CHAPTER 2

"It's a lot nicer when the sun is shining," he says, turning on the lights. "Excuse the mess. I meant to get it cleaned up by the time you came."

We're in a big room with two barred windows on the front looking out onto the trash barrels. The chairs have rumpled sheets thrown over them. There are Indian bedspreads tacked up like curtains. The couch is full of newspapers and toys. There's birdseed or something in the rug. The sink, over on the back wall with the stove and fridge, is piled with dishes. The linoleum has brownish, sticky stains where stuff has spilled and dried.

It's gross, in other words.

"Go on and make yourself comfortable while I get these guys to the bathroom," Dad says. "Put your things anywhere you can find a place."

It's not like Grandma's house is a palace. I've never thought much about whether it's nice or not. It's just home. And it might have a couple thousand too many knickknacks, and dog hairs on the furniture, not to mention the beetles, but the plants aren't all shriveled, and it's neat. Until five minutes ago I'd have said too neat.

The only neat place here is the corner with Dad's music stuff: his keyboards, his amps, two electric guitars on guitar stands, an acoustic guitar, a drum kit, bongos, a box full of rhythm instruments, two music stands. That stuff is all lined up and dusted. I hang my jacket on one of the stands and drop my backpack beside it.

"The couch opens up," Dad says when they get back. He sweeps a bunch of trucks and action figures onto the floor. "You've got the TV right here and twenty-four-hour access to the fridge. There's an empty dresser for you and room in the closet." He switches the television to cartoons, settles the kids in front of it, and shows me down a windowless hall to the bathroom, which smells like diapers. I see only three toothbrushes and three towels.

He's in his room making the bed when I come out.

"When does Tammy get home?" I ask.

He finishes straightening the quilt before he answers. "You know how I said the band was taking a breather? Well . . ."—he plumps up a pillow—"we're actually taking a little breather too, Tammy and me. Or maybe I should say she's taking one."

"What?" I sit down on the bed in front of him. "Tammy left you *and* the band broke up? Dad, why didn't you tell us?"

I feel like ten thousand beetles are swarming through my veins.

He doesn't look at me.

"I don't believe it. Dad, that's the second wife who's left you. That's not good. First Mom, and now her? Dad, that is really messed up. That's so messed up," I say again as he shows me the boys' room. The beds are made, but that's about all you can say for it.

We go back to the living room and sit down on the couch. He pulls off his boots. His big toe pokes through one sock.

"When'd she leave?"

"Couple of weeks ago." He sees me eying the mail and stuff on the table, gets up, and starts putting it in a pile.

"Where'd she go?"

"Moved in with my drummer. And I wouldn't mind if you didn't pass on that particular detail to your grandma. In fact, I wouldn't mind if Ma—"

"Don't worry!" I tell him. That's the last thing Grandma needs to hear. My mom left him for a band member too. No wonder he hasn't been calling.

"Hey, life goes on," he says, going to the fridge. "How're you on peanut butter? I can make you a PB and J, or you can have our particular favorite, PF and B. You ever had that? Peanut butter, Marshmallow Fluff, and banana. It's good. I'll make you one. Orange drink okay with you? It's all we got right now."

"Yeah, sure."

I sit there as he slices bananas. He makes a pile of sandwiches, brings the boys theirs, carries ours to the table, pulls off some paper towels to use as napkins, and hands us our drinks. "But enough about me," he says when he finally sits down across from me. "You were saying you had a solo at the Christmas Eve service?"

"Yes. 'O Holy Night.'" I'm wondering if I *should* call Grandma.

"They still have that Ms. Canetto leading the choir? And is Mrs. What's-her-face still teaching chorus at school? The skinny one, with the buck teeth and the hooty voice—"

"Ms. Briggs," I say, since he clearly has his mind set on a normal conversation. "She hates me."

"Hey, she hated me too," he says. "And look where I am today. How could she hate you?"

"She thought I was showing off," I tell him.

"That's why I quit chorus. Because she kept telling me to sing softer. She said I was sticking out."

"You probably were. Like I said. The little girl with the big pipes. Around here we believe in sticking out, right Chazman?" Charlie's finished his sandwich and is sucking on a piece of cloth. He doesn't look up.

"Chaz, put Blankie down now," Dad says. "Show Kira what you do. You wouldn't know it now," he tells me, "but he's a real ham, this little guy. Show her, Charlie. Show Kira how you do it."

Charlie doesn't look at me but he takes the cloth out of his mouth and does a *phttt-phttt* thing with his lips. Then he puffs his cheeks up and slaps the air out of them.

"Thanks, buddy!" Dad goes over and gives him a kiss. "That was great."

Phttt phttt! He does it again. He still doesn't look at me but I can feel him waiting to see what I'll say.

"That was good, Charlie," I tell him. "It was really good."

"You'd think that was just a little kid making funny noises, right?" Dad says. "Wrong. It's called vocal percussion, and it cracks the crowd up every time."

"Crowd? What crowd?" I'm not sure what he's saying.

"In the subway," he says.

"What?" I get it now. It suddenly makes sense why we spent the afternoon down there. "Tell me you're joking, Dad," I say as the ten thousand beetles start swarming again. "You *are* joking?"

"Uh-uh," he says. "We've been doing real well. Chris plays mean bongos and you should hear him sing, Ki. He's got a gift. Just like you. Chris, you feel like showing Ki how you sing?" Chris's eyes are glued to a cartoon. "What do you say, guys? Want to show Kira our act?" He comes back and sits next to me. "Listen to me, Ki." He puts his hand on my arm. "It's something I can do with the boys. I can pick up some money and still have them with me. They enjoy it. They're like you, natural-born performers. They love to sing. Plus, it's a chance to work on my own act. I've been writing songs. Did I tell you that? I've got a ton of them. Chaz, come over here. Chris, go get your bongos. And turn the TV off. We'll show Kira. Guys, come on, I need you to sing Ki a song. I'm serious, Ki," he says, totally ignoring that they're not moving and I'm sitting here shaking my head. "The act's got promise. It's a real crowd pleaser. The only problem I can see is . . . I'm basically an instrumentalist. I'm not that great of a singer." He leans toward me: "Which is why I was thinking . . ."

"What? That I'm going to sing with you? In a subway station? With a cardboard box for money?" I stand up and go over to the window. There's a pile of birdseed on the sill. I sweep it onto the floor. "That's why you invited me here, Dad? You want me to be a panhandler in the subway? I thought it was because you wanted to see me."

"Whoa, whoa!" He comes up behind me, turns me around, and looks into my eyes. "You're making this sound like it was some kind of evil plot. I did want to see you. I want to spend time with you. I want to show you the city."

"The city subway."

"You said you enjoyed it. And what I showed you was not panhandling. It was artists, performers putting on a show. And if people choose to express their appreciation in a monetary way . . . It beats Pine Manor, right? A bunch of old geezers nodding out in their wheelchairs? It'll be an adventure for you. A new venue. Hey!" He tries to smile. "That was a joke. Come on, Ki, stick that Stickles chin back in. You look like your Grandma when you do that. You've seen the talent down there in the stations. They're the best in the city. They're pros. Like me. Or pros in the making. Like you. And did you see any singers? No. Never mind a young girl with a voice like you."

"Oh, right. 'Where'd a little thing like you get such a big voice?'" I coo. "'What an incredible instrument!' 'Sing us a song, Kira!' 'Come on, honey, let me hear you sing.' 'Kira, sing "His Eye Is on the Sparrow."' 'Sing "Somewhere Over the Rainbow."' 'Kira, what was that cute little song you used to sing?'" Now that I've started I can't seem to stop. "'Smile!' 'Give us a smile, sweetheart.' 'Oh, you look *so* much prettier when you smile.' 'You *know,* if you keep frowning like that, one of these days you're going to wake up and find your face has turned into a prune.'" I drop the phony voices. "And if their little incredible instrument doesn't feel like smiling or singing, they're all, like, 'What's *her* problem? Whoa, that Kira's got an attitude!'" I'm so mad my ears are floating. "I'm not a human jukebox, Dad, or a dancing doll, or a puppet where you press a button and I'll entertain you. And neither are the boys!"

"Slow down, Kira," he says. "Nobody's saying you've got an attitude. All I'm saying is your voice is as good as your mother's."

That stops me dead.

"What?" My mom sang with Dad's band. Everyone says she was an amazing singer. I know I look like her. But he's never said . . . No. Forget it. No way. I'm not going there.

He sounds so sincere, though.

"Russell always sounds sincere," I can just hear Grandma saying. "It's his specialty. That, and dreaming, and baloney."

And now he's singing.

> *"Seems like some folks do the leaving*
> *And some folks are the left.*
> *I don't know why it works that way,*
> *I guess it's for the best.*
> *But I just can't help this aching—"*

"Dad!" I cut him off. "Don't do this to me."

"I wrote that," he says. "I wrote it Christmas day."

I stay by the window with my arms folded while he cleans up from dinner and then takes the kids in to wash up for bed. I sit there when he brings them to their bedroom for a story.

"Kira!" he calls. "Want to come in and give the guys a good-night kiss?"

"No," I say. But I get up and go to their room. They're under the covers. Charlie's sucking on his blankie. Chris has an action figure in each hand. They look so little. I lean over and give them each a kiss. "Good night, guys."

They don't answer.

"I'm sorry, Ki," Dad says once we're back in the living room. "I shouldn't have dumped all this on you. Now I've got you upset." He looks like Jimmy the dog when he's dug up the flower bed and Grandma's given him what for. "I hear what you're saying. And it's fine. I'm cool with it." When I don't answer, he adds, "And I promise I won't ask you to smile."

We sit there not saying anything until he says, "Listen, kiddo, can I ask you a very big favor? A really big favor? Don't worry"—he still looks like Jimmy—"it has nothing to do with subways. Or singing. I have not been away from these kids for five minutes since Tammy took off. Would you mind if I go out just for a little bit? I could really use a break."

"What?" I say. "And I stay here? Alone?"

"Just for a few minutes," he says. "It's not even eight o'clock. I just need to take a walk around the block or something. The boys are in bed. You'll be perfectly safe. And I'll be right back. Five, ten minutes."

He stands up.

I try to keep my voice calm. "How 'bout if you stay here now, and you have a break tomorrow? You can go out for as long as you want tomorrow. In the daytime." I have another idea. He'll hate it. I don't care. "Or tomorrow we'll go back home. You can stay with us. With Grandma and me. You can stay as long as—"

"Ten minutes, honey," he says, walking toward the door. "Fifteen, max. I just need some air. I swear to God. I'll be right back. You're still hungry, right?"

"No!" I say.

"Shhh!" He puts his finger to his lips. "They may still be awake. I'll bring us back some ice cream." He takes his jacket off the doorknob and puts it on.

I grab his arm. "Dad. You can't leave them with me. They'll freak. They hardly know me."

"They know you," he says. "You're their sister. *Dulce de leche.* You never had that, right? I know they don't sell that in Claryville. You'll love it."

And then he's out the door, locking it behind him. Locking the gate.

"Dad!" I yell after him. "I don't know how the locks work. I don't even have the keys."

He's gone.

CHAPTER 3

Chris and Charlie are standing in the doorway to the living room. Charlie is crying. "I want my daddy!"

"Where'd Dad go?" Chris whines. "When's Dad coming back? Where's my dad?"

It's the first time they've spoken to me all day. I don't know how to answer them.

"He'll be back in a few minutes," I say. I can hear an ambulance wailing somewhere down the street and two women arguing as they walk by the windows. I make my voice like Grandma's Pine Manor voice. "Get back in bed, boys."

"No," Charlie says.

I make my face like Grandma's when she talks to the residents who are a little confused. "Sweetie pie, we're going back to bed now."

"I want to get in Chris's bed," Charlie says.

"Fine," I say. "Get in Chris's bed."

"With Chris," he says.

"No way!" Chris yells. "He wets the bed."

"He doesn't wear diapers?"

"No," Charlie says.

"You do too!" Chris says.

"Charlie"—I'm still trying to sound like Grandma—"do you need a diaper?"

"No," he says again. He looks like he wants to kill both of us.

Chris looks like he thinks I've never put a diaper on anyone and have no clue how it's done. Which is true. "I want my dad," he says.

The phone must be in Dad's room. I haven't seen one in the living room or the kitchen. I can't decide if I need Grandma to drive down this minute or if I'll just ask her what to do.

"Where are you going?" Chris calls after me.

"I need to make a call," I say. "Where's the phone?"

"Don't have one," he says.

"What?" I stop walking.

"He had it turned off. He said people were bothering him."

"And there's no cell phone or anything?"

He shakes his head. "Uh-uh."

Well, now I won't have to tell Grandma she was right about Dad.

Since I can't think of anything else to do, I go back to the boys' room, kick off my sneakers, get in

Chris's bed, and pull the covers up. Both boys are watching me.

"Can I get in with you?" Chris says.

I move over to make room for him. He climbs in.

"Can I?" Charlie says.

"You're not going to pee on me?"

"No," he says, but it's a different "no," so I say "Sure," and he gets in too.

I pull the covers over all of us. They lie there stiff as boards, staring at the ceiling, Chris clutching his action figures, Charlie holding tight to his blankie. I'm clutching Grandma's horseshoe charm necklace, running my thumb over the tiny diamonds. I couldn't believe it this morning when she took it off from around her neck and put it on me. "You'll want something special to wear," she said. "In case they take you out somewhere nice." *Right.*

"Now what?" Chris says.

"I don't know." I'm squashed up against the wall. It's hot in here. The pillow—the small piece of it I have—is already hot. The radiator sounds like it's going to blow itself apart. "Go to sleep."

"Dad always sings us a funny song," Charlie says. He seems like he's about to cry. Chris might be too. I don't dare look, but I hear sniffles.

"I don't know any funny songs," I tell him. All I

can think of is that stupid song of Mr. Corrigan's: *The worms crawl in, the worms crawl out. The worms play pinochle on your snout.* "Just go to sleep, okay? Don't cry. Please." If they cry, I'll cry.

I put an arm around each of them. And then a song pops into my head. Not a funny song.

A song my mom used to sing.

> *"Hush-a-bye, don't you cry,*
> *Go to sleepy, little baby."*

I haven't thought about that song in so long.

> *"When you wake, you'll have cake,*
> *And all the pretty little horses."*

She sang that to me a lot.

At first I'm not sure I remember the words, but when I start singing it, I do. I sing real soft so I can hear if Dad comes back. Or if anyone's trying to break down the door and kill us.

> *"Black and bay, dapple and gray . . ."*

I used to think it was *dabble*. I still don't know what *bay* is. I mumble those words so Chris and

Charlie won't ask. Because they're listening to me. I wouldn't call them relaxed—they're still basically stiff as boards—but they're listening hard.

And now I'm at the verse that always creeped me out, the one about a lamb crying for its mommy while bees and butterflies pick out its eyes. She always tried to skip that verse so we wouldn't get into a whole thing about whether the lamb was alive or dead, because then I wouldn't go to sleep, but I made her sing it every time. I skip over it now and go "*doo doo doo*" instead.

It seems to be working. The boys aren't totally rigid.

I'm still rigid. I keep singing. I sing it over and over. Even when I think they're almost asleep, I keep singing. But each time I get to that dead lamb, even though I'm still just going "*doo doo doo*," my voice catches in my throat.

And then, finally, Dad is standing in the door-way, giving me the thumbs-up.

"Look at that," he whispers, shaking his head. He signals me to come over to him. I want to jump out of bed and start yelling at him—either that or punch him in the nose—but since the boys really are asleep now, I ease out carefully and tiptoe over.

"I knew you'd do it," he says, putting his arm

around me, giving me a squeeze. "The woman's touch, that's what these guys needed. And that little walk was just what I needed. I got us the ice cream." He unzips his jacket and pulls out a pint of *dulce de leche.* "I kept it right in here, right under my arm, so it would soften up on the way and you wouldn't have to wait. A little ice cream sound good to you?"

"No." I wonder if he's shoplifted it. "No." Nothing sounds good at the moment except being home.

"You say that now," he says as I follow him to the kitchen. "Just wait till you try it." He pulls bowls and two spoons from the sink, washes them, and dries them on a towel. He's looking at me like he's waiting for something. If it's for me to offer to do his dishes, he's going to have a long wait.

"You left me here alone," I tell him. "Without a phone."

"I said I'd be right back," he says, "and here I am." He's turned on the water and is putting some dish soap on the pile. "Okay. You're pissed. I can appreciate that. And you're thinking I'm full of baloney."

"That's right."

"You're thinking I'm so full of baloney, I've got baloney squirting out my ears."

"That's right," I say again. "And I'm not going to laugh, Dad, so you can quit trying."

"That's cool. You don't have to laugh." He's stopped looking at me. "I know this is not the way either of us would like it, but you think you can bear with me here a little, Ki?"

"Why would I do that?" I say.

"Honestly?" he says. "I don't know. But I wish you would."

The Can of Worms

Jake didn't plan on cutting English. His feet just took one step inside Mintzer's door, said *I don't think so*, turned around, and kept on going. So then why is he still running? He's blocks from school already. It's unlikely Ms. Mintzer even noticed him come in, never mind saw him walk out. At first he thought he'd stay out only till the end of English and slip back for seventh and eighth periods—computer science, with Eugene, then study hall. Now he's thinking, home.

Of course, his dad might be at home working. And even though if anyone would understand, it would be Jake's dad, his dad is sure to point out that it's somewhat dumb to read the book, write the report—which he knows Jake did—and then bury it in his binder till it's so late Jake's lucky if he gets a C-minus. It might be dumb, but it's been working: You hold on to something till the teacher has given up on seeing it, is sick to death of listening to oral reports, and you don't have to present. Till yesterday, when Ms. Mintzer walked around collecting book reports and he sat there with his head down, and his heart pounding, and the report in his binder, and she stood by his desk, and he didn't say anything, and she said, "Jake, I'm waiting," and he didn't say anything, and she said, "Jake, your book report please. You do have it, don't you?" and he said nothing, and she said, "You know, Jake, that's four you've turned in late now. Jake, you had all of winter break to work on it. Jake, we need to talk," and he said, *Easy for you to say*.

Or would have, if he could have.

He's almost at the subway station before he realizes he's not running because he's freaked. He's running because he's out of there and he can breathe, and breathing feels good. He thinks about running all the way home. But when he goes down into the subway and hears the singing, he is so glad he didn't.

It's not just his daring Mintzer escape. Or that his mood always lifts when he hears music in the subway. Jake's never heard a voice like this before. It carries all the way down the platform, yet it seems effortless: "Hey, Jude, don't make it bad . . ." As he gets nearer he hears a guitar behind her, and little-kid voices. When he's close enough to see, he's even more amazed. He was sure it was a grown woman. It's a kid, a girl his age, in jeans and a too-big denim jacket and this funky-looking feather thing. She's singing with a man in a cruddy motor-cycle jacket, and with two little boys with mittens hanging from their sleeves on bongos and a tam-bourine. There's a guitar case open in front of them for money.

Jake finds a spot over by the wall, and when the song ends he claps. A homeless man claps. A woman drops a dollar bill in the guitar case.

"Thank you," the dad says. "Thank you so much." He has to be the dad. He looks just like her— small and thin, with pointy features and curly, red-dish hair. His hair's as long as hers, but it's in a ponytail. The back of his head is bald. "God bless you," he says. "Appreciate the support."

The girl begins to sing again, alone this time, without even the guitar. "Me and Bobby McGee." Jake likes the way she eases into it, as if she's singing to herself, just letting the rest of the world listen in. She sings till the number 1 local rattles to a stop. Then she picks up a bottle of water, takes a drink, and passes it to the little guys.

He was hoping she'd go back to "Bobby McGee" when the train pulls out. But her dad says something to her, she nods, the dad picks up his guitar and plays the intro to "I Will Always Love You," which Jake doesn't like. The way her voice soars up though, clear and sweet, but not that wobbly, warbly, whiny sweet . . .

Jake moves a few feet closer, slips off his backpack, and leans against a pillar.

"Mmmph!" A man standing near him shakes his head. "That little girl can sing! You've got some voice, honey," he tells her, stepping up and throwing a dollar into the guitar case.

The dad nods and thanks him.

"I haven't seen you here before," a woman tells her. "I hope I'll see you here again."

"Oh, you will," the dad says. "You surely will."

Other people walk up and speak to them too. It's always the dad who answers. The girl just stands there and sings. Sometimes singing the songs straight, the dad singing harmony or not; other times taking off from what he's doing on the guitar, playing with the melody or the rhythm, adding swoops and dips and riffs. Jake stays through more "Hey, Jude"s, more "I Will Always Love You"s, more "Amazing Grace"s.

A couple of times he thinks he sees the girl glancing at him, but she looks away fast. The little boys, meanwhile, have had enough of this. The bigger one hops off his plastic crate and gets a bag of Cheez Doodles from their shopping cart. The one in the stroller keeps dropping his tambourine and climbing out to get it and the dad has to keep putting him back in, which makes the boy cry. The dad gives him a pacifier. The boy throws it on the ground. A woman picks it up.

"Make sure you wash that before he puts it in his mouth again," she scolds the dad.

"Don't worry, ma'am," he says. "See, it's goin' right here in my pocket."

"Passy!" The boy cries even louder. The woman walks away without giving them any money.

The dad's smile fades. "Have a nice day," he calls after her. "Appreciate the support. God bless you."

Through all of this, the girl just sings. *What could that feel like,* Jake wonders, *to stand in front of strangers and open your mouth and have sounds like that come out? To open your mouth and feel no fear?* It's how he would sing, if he had a voice. A real voice, that is. Not just inside his head.

But thinking that gets him thinking about school again, worrying about Mintzer. Which he's still doing when three men carrying instrument cases come toward them. It's the tuba trio. Old guys. Eugene loves these guys. He and Eugene have seen them in a bunch of stations.

"I'm sorry, sir," one of them tells the dad as they set their cases down and unfold their Music Under New York banner. "We're gonna have to ask you to leave. We've got this spot from two to five."

"It's okay," the dad tells the girl. "Keep singing, honey. We'll work this out. No offense, my friend," he tells the guy. "But we were here first."

"True enough," the tuba guy says. "But these spots are assigned. You can play anywhere you want if no one's here, but unless you've got a permit from the city . . ."

"You're kidding," the dad tells him. "Listen. We're new at this. Just blew into town. You know what they say, right? If you can make it here, you can make it anywhere. We're not doin' too bad so far," he says, nodding toward the guitar case, "but to tell you the truth, I was kinda hopin' for one more song."

The tuba guy checks his watch. "Sure. Why not? We can give you five minutes. Knock yourself out."

"'Preciate it," the dad says. He turns to Jake. "Got a request? This kid's been standing here listening to my daughter for an hour," he tells the tuba guys. "It's your big chance, man," he tells Jake. "What do you want to hear?"

Jake wants to hear "Me and Bobby McGee." But he hasn't planned for this. *M*s are trouble. It has to be a really good day not to block on *M*s. *B*s are death. And the boy with the bongos is tugging on the dad's leg, going "Dad, let's go," and the dad's standing there, waiting for Jake to say something, and the girl's looking at him, and she's waiting, too. *Would you stop looking at me?* Jake wants to shout. *It's not helping!*

He thinks about asking for "I Will Always Love You" because vowels are easier, and once he's gotten through the "I Will," he can push through the rest. Except that she's sung it at least five times. And he hates the song. He could try an end run, around the "Bobby" and the "McGee," to that line from the middle: "Freedom's just another word for nothing left to lose."

Except now *F*s aren't working either.

If Eugene were here he'd jump in for Jake, make a joke about Killer *B*s, say, "There will be a brief pause for technical difficulties," or, "Words fail him." Something to break the tension.

Jake's face feels like it's going to explode.

The tuba guy checks his watch again. "Hey, I

know she's good, man," he tells Jake, "but get a grip. If you want a song you're gonna have to talk to her."

Don't you think I know that? Jake wants to shout. *Do I look stupid?*

"Hey. It's a'right," the tuba guy says, holding up his hand. "I'm joking, man. Take it easy. Slow down. Deep breath. Relax. Count to ten. You can do it, buddy."

No. If I could do it, I'd be doing it.

Jake picks up his backpack. He's all set to walk away when she starts to sing, the same as the other time, soft and quiet, like she's all alone. He doesn't dare look up, so he can't know if she's looking his way, but that's fine with him. She's singing "Me and Bobby McGee."

CHAPTER 5

That night Jake dreams he's on a stage. "Thank you, thank you so much," he tells the cheering crowd. "I'm Jake Kandell and I'm excited you all could make it here tonight."

He knows it's a dream even while he's dreaming it because he can say "thank you" without getting tripped up by the *Th*s. Even his name slides out effortlessly. But this dream doesn't end the usual way, with his feeling a cold breeze on his butt and realizing he's left home without his pants, then looking up to find he's in Yankee Stadium, and President Lincoln can't throw out the first ball of the season till Jake's recited the Gettysburg Address, then waking up pissed because who needs a dream if it's going to be bad. *Uh-uh*. In this dream Jake sings. And he is *good*.

The song is gone as soon as he wakes up. But the dream is so real that even when he gets to school, when he sees the sign posted in the hall—IS THERE A SINGER INSIDE YOU TRYING TO GET OUT? CHORUS IS WELCOMING

NEW MEMBERS—he actually thinks, *Hmmm. . . .* It doesn't totally wipe away the *Get me out of here!* he's also feeling, but it helps him make it through to lunch.

"So let me get this straight," Eugene says as he and Jake take their trays to their usual spot at the last table in the back, over by the trash cans. "You stomped out of Mintzer's class and met a beautiful, mysterious singing goddess, and I missed it?"

"I didn't say she was beautiful," Jake tells him. Though she was, almost, when she sang. "It was her voice."

"You gonna go look for her again today after lunch?" Eugene asks. "I'd cut with you, but . . ." He makes a face.

"Don't worry about it." Even if Eugene were willing, Jake doesn't dare cut two days in a row. He just wishes Eugene had English with him, so he didn't have to face Ms. Mintzer alone.

On Jake's good days, Ms. Mintzer just seems like an oldish and somewhat fat teacher with a grating voice and ugly black glasses who refuses to leave him alone—unlike his other teachers, who love that he's quiet, who are thrilled to have him sit in the back and do his work and not give them any lip.

Jake can't remember too many good days lately. When he was younger, he used to think there was a little demon guy who lived in the light fixture above his kitchen table. Good days, the Evil Tongue God would just sort of hang out up there and mind his business. Bad days, though, down he'd swing on his little rope with his little bag of tools onto Jake's back, just far enough down so Jake could never catch a glimpse of him or knock him off, or know when he was about to sneak up and clamp Jake's jaws closed, or grab Jake by the tongue with his little pliers.

Jake spent years trying to figure out what made some days good days, looking for ways to trick the tongue god, or outsmart him, or make deals with him: *Let me say my name this one time and I'll eat my eggplant,* that sort of thing. Avoiding the chair under the light fixture. Avoiding all light fixtures. Devising special anti-Evil Tongue God charms. The only thing guaranteed to work was to keep his mouth shut.

Which helps him not a bit with Ms. Mintzer.

"I missed you in class yesterday," she says, leaning over Jake's desk so that he can smell the tuna fish she had for lunch. "You're the only one who hasn't presented, Jake. You do have your book report ready today, don't you?"

"I . . . uh . . . I . . . I . . ." *Forgot it* is what he wants to say. "I . . . uh . . . s-s-s-seem t-t-t . . . I . . . uh . . . ap-p-p-p-pear n-n-n-not . . ."

"Okay, Jake," she says. "We won't take up class time with this now. Come by and see me at three o'clock."

At three o'clock he meets Eugene. There are four different middle schools in the building. Instead of going out their regular ground-floor exit, they run up the back stairs to the first floor and out the main doors so Jake won't have to pass Mintzer's room and they can disappear into the stream of kids pouring out onto the street.

The subway station is packed with kids eating pizza, flirting, being loud. Jake nods to the ones he knows, but he's relieved when Eugene doesn't try to talk to them. He doesn't hear any music today. The only performer seems to be the statue lady on her silver pedestal, with her silver hood, tight silver bodysuit, and silver makeup on her face and hands. One arm is by her side. The other's raised up, as if she got turned to silver while waving to her fans. That's all she does, just stands there, smiling, frozen.

Eugene pulls his arms up into his sleeves so that the sleeve bottoms hang free. Then he twirls them up and flaps them loose. He's doing that, studying the statue lady, when two girls and a boy from school come up beside them. Jake doesn't know them. He's hoping they don't know him. They do seem to know Eugene.

"It's Eugene Kim," the pink-haired girl says with a smirk. "Hel*lo,* Eu*geeeene*! What are you doing?"

Leaving, is what Jake wants to say. *Departing. Exiting.* But before he can decide on the safest word to try, the nonpink one chimes in: "Think you can get her to move, Eu*geeeene*?"

"Him? Nah," the boy says. They're all smirking now.

Eugene steps up to the statue lady, reaches in his pocket, and pulls out a box of Nik Nak breath mints. Eugene is never without Nik Naks. "Nik Nak?" he offers. She doesn't budge. "Hel*lo*! And *wel*come to Subway Land!" he says in a Moviefone Man voice. He switches to a Transylvanian accent. "How do you do, my little chickadee?" Her eyelids don't even flicker. He drops the Dracula voice. "Have you noticed that nobody says 'how do you do' anymore? Why is that?" He steps closer. "Uh-oh! There's something on your nose. I think it might be a mosquito. No, it's a gnat. A guh-nat. A gee-nat. A small, annoying insect." He sees Jake giving him warning looks. "My friend here says I am a small, annoying insect. Do you agree?"

Still nothing. Jake doesn't get why the statue

lady is doing this. You couldn't pay him enough to stand there and have people try to taunt a response out of him. And it has to be pissing off Eugene having these three smirkers going, "Told you." "Give up, Eu*geeene*." "You just don't have the touch."

"Oh, yeah?" Jake says. It's lamer than he wants, but he gets it out.

Eugene shoots him a grateful look, then goes into a gigantic yawn. The statue lady doesn't even blink. He pretends to sneeze. Nothing.

"I hate to break it to you, schweetheart," he tells her. "I think you may be dead."

It's possible the girls are laughing with him. Jake can't tell. "To be, or not to be: that is the question," Eugene quacks in a Donald Duck voice. The girls laugh some more. The statue lady hasn't moved a muscle.

"You're good," Eugene says, pulling his hand out of his sleeve to salute her. "Have a nice day."

As he and Jake start to leave, she winks at Jake and blows Eugene a kiss.

"See? Piece of cake!" Eugene tells the kids. "Whew!" he whispers to Jake as they walk away.

"You know, you c-c-c-could try the l-l-l-low p-p-p-profile approach once in a while," Jake says as they move down the platform. "You don't have to . . ." He stops. He's hearing the "I Will Always Love You" intro. Then he hears the girl's voice, soaring up and up. They're way at the far end today.

"That's her?" Eugene says.

Jake nods. When they get about ten feet away, he makes Eugene stop. "L-L-L-Low p-p-p . . . p-p-p . . . ," he tries to say again. *Why is this happening?* Eugene's usually the one person he can talk to. With Eugene he's almost glitchless. He takes in a deep breath and lets out the *S*: "S-S-S-Silence, okay?"

"Yes, my liege." Eugene bows, then reaches in his pocket and offers him a Nik Nak.

Jake shakes his head. He still hates this song, but she is so good.

"Yo!" Eugene pokes him. "Jake. She's looking at you."

"No, she's not." A woman with earrings the size of basketball hoops is blocking her view. "Sh-Sh-Sh-She can't even see us." He hasn't decided yet if he wants her to.

"She senses your presence," Eugene says. "She feels your aura." He starts singing along with her. "'And I-*eee*-I will awwwl-wayzzz . . .'" Even when he's not trying to sing, his voice reminds Jake of a sea lion. *If he starts flapping his sleeves, someone might throw him a fish.* Jake clamps his hand over

Eugene's mouth and holds it there till the song ends.

"Hey, if you can't spare a dollar, give us a smile," the dad calls to people as they pass. "Smile! It costs you nothing and it won't mess up your hair." He nods to the smaller boy, who shakes his tambourine, and they start "Amazing Grace." The girl's voice is smooth and easy, like water. Or floating through water. Jake moves a little closer.

Eugene moves a lot closer. "Amazing Grace," he says to the girl when the song ends. "Grace the Amazing. Is that by any chance your name? Because you are amazing."

"No. It isn't," she says into the mike. It's the first thing Jake's heard her say.

Her dad takes the mike from her. "But thank you all the same," he tells Eugene. "Nice to see you again, buddy," he says to Jake. "How you doin' today?"

Eugene comes to the rescue. "What *is* your name, if you don't mind my asking?"

"Oh, go on," the dad says when the girl doesn't answer. "Tell your fans what your name is." He winks at her, then takes the mike. "It's . . . ummm . . . Cleo." He gives her another wink. "Short for Cleopatra."

"Amazing Cleo," Eugene says. "And you would be how old?"

The dad throws her a look. "Sixteen."

"Sixteen?" Eugene shakes his head. "No way. Of course that only makes you more amazing. . . ."

Jake peers down the track for a train. Nothing coming. What he does see are the smirkers, headed right for them.

"Eu*geeene*! We meet again," the pink-haired girl says.

"Who you hittin' on now?" the boy says.

"This is Amazing Cleo," Eugene announces.

"And these are my two sons"—the dad points to the boys—"Amazing Christopher and Amazing Charles, and I'm Russell Stickles, hopefully amazing, and you're Eugene, and . . ." Jake's heart stops as he waits for the dad to ask his name. There's still no train coming. "Speaking of hopefully amazing," the dad says, "we've got some original material for you today, written by yours truly. Chazman, come on over here and give us a little vocal percussion so your sister can take a break."

He hands the boy his pacifier. The boy sticks it in his mouth. Cleo takes the older kid by the hand and moves over to a pillar. Russell picks up the guitar and plays a bluesy intro, then starts to sing. Jake hasn't heard him sing alone. He's got one of those rough, scratchy rock-singer voices.

"A bad song is better than no song. Don't
  you know,
A sad song beats no song at all."

He nods to the little boy, who pulls his pacifier out of his mouth like he's yanking a bathtub plug. It makes a loud pop.

"And maybe that sad song ain't really so
  sad."

Pop!

"And maybe your mad girl ain't totally
  mad."

Pop!

"And long as you're singing or playing a riff,
I doubt you'll be flinging yourself off a cliff."

"What?" Eugene says. "Is he for real?" He starts imitating the popping noises. Meanwhile, Pink and her friends are rolling their eyes and laughing, at the dad and at Eugene—there's no doubt in Jake's mind now that they're laughing at him, not with him—and the dad is still singing, about lovin' and oven, and edge and ledge, and Jake's trying to ignore all of it, but there's no way.

> *"Tell that girl she's your treasure and sing*
>   *one more measure,*
> *Then sing it again, and again, and again,*
> *'Cause a bad song—"*

"Talk about bad songs!" Eugene says, loud enough for everyone to hear. A group of high school kids walking by nods and laughs.

The woman with the earrings turns and glares at him. *"Excuse me!"* Her voice has the rich, rolling ring of TV commercials for antidepressants or life insurance, or like the voice of God in cartoons, if they used a woman. "That's *very* rude."

Eugene makes a face. "Sorry."

Pink and her friends snicker.

Jake's so embarrassed for Cleo he hardly dares look at her, but there she is, still holding the kid's hand, with the same untouchable look she had when she was singing, like it all slides off her, if she even notices. At last, finally, the express rumbles in, drowning out everything. Jake grabs Eugene by the arm and they get on.

They've gone several stops without saying anything when Eugene says, "So I guess you're mad at me."

"No," Jake says.

"Because I've got a new line for old Russell Stickles. Wanna hear?"

"Not really."

Eugene sings it anyway: "But in his case, the song is so wack, I've decided to throw his guitar on the track."

A minute later he asks: "So, are we gonna hang out?"

"I'm not in the m-m-m-mood," Jake says. But then, because he knows how Eugene hates spending all afternoon and evening at his parents' store, he adds, "Sorry."

"Sure you don't need me to help hold Leona down?" Eugene asks.

"Nah, it's fine. I'll be fine."

"Come on, Leona. That's a good girl. This'll only take a minute."

Jake sits on the kitchen floor with the cat clamped between his legs and the medicine bottles off to the side so she won't knock them over if she makes a run for it. "So how was your day, Leona?" he asks as he tightens his knee hold. Jake can talk perfectly to Leona. Or any nonhuman. "What's new and exciting in the cat world?" He smoothes the cat's head. "What'll we do first today, eyes or ears?"

He squirts some gunk in and folds her ear closed. "Hey, cat, don't make it bad," he sings to the tune of "Hey, Jude" as he rubs the stuff around. "Take your eardrops, they'll make you better." *Not bad. Not like in the dream, and nothing like the subway girl, but better than Russell.* Leona seems to like it. "Remember to keep it under your tongue," he sings as he puts an eyedrop in each eye. "It helps your lung and gets you bet-ter." She's not flinching and twisting as much as usual. He could swear it's his singing. He pries open her mouth and sings some more: "Oh, capsules are more aerodynamic than pills. They slide down your thro-oat a whole lot better. Nah-nah-nah-nah, nah-nah-nah-naaah!" She doesn't even try to bite him.

Sometimes Jake thinks he should be an exterminator when he grows up, or a mortician, since you don't need to talk to cockroaches or corpses. Now, as Leona settles into his lap, purring, and he rubs under her chin and around her ears, he thinks, *Animal trainer? Vet? Pet therapist?*

"And I-*eee*-I will alwwwayzzz love you-oo-ooh . . . will alwwwayzzz scratch you, pet you, oo-ooh."

His dad comes in. "I'm going for a run," he says. "You want to join me?"

"Sure," Jake says.

He stands up and carries Leona to the corner and sets her down by the heat riser. Then they change and head out to Riverside Park.

"So, uh, uh, how'd your day go?" his dad says once they've started to run. "Anything good happen?"

"No," Jake says. "How 'b-b-b-bout you?"

"You know, the, uh, the, uh, usual," Dad says.

Jake always tells himself that if he can only wait it out, his speech will get to where his dad's is, where people just think he talks extra carefully and has blips or slips here and there. Or that the problem might simply disappear. Evaporate. Vanish. He sometimes thinks about asking Dad how that worked with him, but stuttering—Dad's, his, anyone's—is not something they talk about.

They run through the park, then cut down under the highway to the bike path along the river. It's cold and almost dark. Jake doesn't care. It's so nice down here with the lights sparkling across the river and the George Washington Bridge lit up like a Christmas tree and chunks of ice bobbing in the water. He likes the sting of the wind on his face. He likes feeling the rhythm of his feet. He wishes he could run and run and run.

"I Suppose This Is Good News"

"America, America, God shared his grapes with me. . . ."

It's Friday, my eighth day in the subway. It feels like eight weeks.

The morning rush is over. Dad's let Chris and Charlie have the mike. Charlie's too little to do much, but Chris is great. "And drown thy good . . . ," Chris sings. A subway worker looks up from her sweeping and gives us a smile.

"Hey, Feathers! Feathers, whassup?" Two boys in puffy black jackets stop in front of us. The taller one's wearing big jeans. The shorter one looks like he forgot to get dressed. They're both taller than me, but they look young. "Yo, Feathers," the one in pajamas calls to me. "You need to teach your little brother the words."

I flip my scarf around my neck and keep singing harmony. Chris knows the words. He just likes his better. When he finishes the song, the subway worker claps. Dad leans over and gives both boys a kiss, hands me back the mike, and we start it again, this time with me singing.

The two kids move in closer. "You sing here every day?" the one in the pajamas asks. "So how much money you make?" He peers in the guitar case. "Whoa! They're rakin' it in. We should do this too, you know," he tells his friend. "I can sing as good as her." He spreads his arms like an opera singer. "For purple mountain's majesty. . . ." He sounds like a cow with gas pains. His friend laughs.

I'm still trying to ignore them. It's the only way. Forget the people. Especially the kids. Except for that boy who got all tongue-tied, the cute-looking one with the chubby friend. Let Dad do the talking. Dad can talk and play without losing a beat. He likes talking to people. It doesn't get to him.

We finish "America the Beautiful" as the 1 train pulls in. *Bing-bong!* The doors open. I wait for the kids to get on. They don't.

Dad rolls his eyes at me. "Hey, guys," he says. "No offense, but don't you have someplace you're supposed to be?"

The jeans one shrugs. "Nuh-uh. We're enjoying the show."

"You should tell Feathers to smile more, though," the pajama one tells Dad. "Better for business."

Better for business if you minded your business, I want to say, but Dad gives me his "Chill, Ki" look, and says, "Thank you. Appreciate the input."

When the train leaves he starts the intro to "I Believe I Can Fly." We worked up the arrangement last night. We taught Chris a bongo part, gave Charlie enough to do on his tambourine so he won't make too many mouth noises and make people laugh, then practiced till it got good. It's not a song I like, but then neither are most of the songs we're doing.

"I Believe I Can Fly," Dad announces.

"I believe I can, too," Jeans says, flapping his arms. The pajama kid snickers and starts the gaseous routine again. He seems to think he's imitating me. Jeans laughs harder and begins doing a chicken dance, singing *"Pawk, pawk"* instead of the words.

"Do you mind?" Dad says to them. "We're putting on a show here, okay?"

"We're putting on a show too," the pajama kid says. "It's a free country, right, Feathers?" I pretend I don't hear him. "What, you can't say nothin'?" he says, then turns to his friend. "Feathers thinks she's too good to talk to us."

"A stink beetle is too good to talk to you, Pajama Pants," I say into the mike. "And you better hold on to those jeans," I tell his friend. "Before you lose them."

I shouldn't have said anything. Jeans grabs the end of my scarf and yanks it off my neck. I reach for it. He dances away and hands it to Pajama Pants, who steps to the edge of the platform and dangles it over the tracks, hollering, "You want it, Feathers? Come get it!"

I'm about to. Dad holds me back and hands me his guitar. "Listen, you little punks!" he yells as he takes off after them. "You want to mess with someone, mess with me. Keep away from my daughter!"

"Yeah, you little punks!" Charlie runs around to his stroller bag, pulls out this little three-inch plastic action-figure sword and hands it to me. "Now you can get them, Ki!" he says. His eyes are scared, though.

Chris looks even more scared. "Dad, come back!" he screams. "Kiki"—he tugs on my leg—"make him come back. He's too close to the edge!"

I take both their hands. "He'll be okay." I try to make my voice like Grandma's. Pajama Pants dodges between people, ducking behind pillars, laughing, as Dad runs after him. I want Dad to catch him, but I'm terrified they'll get into a fight. Or that a train will come, and they'll jump on with my scarf, and he'll chase after them and leave us here. "Forget the scarf, Dad!" I shout to him. "Let them have it."

"I'll let 'em have it all right!" he yells back.

"Oh, yeah?" Pajama Pants darts out from behind a pillar and waves the scarf.

"Yeah!" Dad pushes past some people, grabs him by his hood, and snatches the scarf.

"Watch out!" I scream as Jeans runs up behind him. Chris and Charlie are clutching my hands.

Dad wheels around, sticks out his foot and trips him. Jeans falls on the platform, cursing. They're all cursing up a storm.

Pajama Pants has his arm cocked to punch Dad when two cops appear. One grabs Pajama Pants. The other pulls Jeans to his feet. "Okay," he says. "What's goin' on?"

"They stole my daughter's scarf," Dad says. His face is red and sweaty. He has to bend over to catch his breath. "I got it back," he says, handing it to me.

"We didn't steal it," Pajama Pants says. "I was playin' with her, that's all. I was about to give it back. But then this crazy homeless dude here starts chasing—"

"Never mind him," the cop says. "Why aren't you two in school? Let me see your IDs."

The boys fumble around and pull out cards. The cop looks the cards over, then turns to Pajama Pants. "Where's your mother, Robert?"

He looks down at his shoes. "At work."

"She know you're cutting school today, Robert? What about you, Jeffrey? Your mother know you're not in school?"

"I don't know. No."

"You know her number?"

"Yeah."

"Give it to me. We're gonna call her right now. Yours, too, Robert." He leads the boys down the platform.

"Are they taking them to jail?" Chris whispers to me. "Is Dad going to jail too? Are we, Kiki?"

"No," I say in my Grandma voice. "It'll be okay, Chris. No one's going to jail."

But a second later I'm not so sure. The other cop is asking Dad for his driver's license. He studies it a long time, then nods toward Chris and Charlie. "These your children, Russell?" They're still clutching my hands.

"Yes, officer," Dad says. "Is there a problem? I'm allowed to perform here, right? The way I understand it, I'm within my rights."

"Not if you're causing a disturbance." He's talking to Dad the same way he talked to those kids. Like he's deaf. And stupid. "Your daughter's supposed to be in school too. How old is she?"

"Thirteen," I say before Dad can answer. "And we're not homeless."

The cop steps closer to me. "What school do you go to?"

"She's just down here on a visit, officer," Dad answers. "For the holidays. Her school don't start till Monday. She's going back."

I was about to tell them that. I dig out the name tag Grandma made for me and show the cop. It has nothing about my school but it has my upstate address and phone. I pray he doesn't ask for Grandma's work number. Though part of me hopes he does.

He takes forever to look at it. "I've seen you here before, Russell," he says finally. "I've seen you people in other stations too. You shouldn't be bringing these kids down here. They should be in day care." He's got his finger almost in Dad's face.

A woman who's been watching nods. She says something to the man next to her. He starts gawking too.

"I don't want to see you down here with them again," the cop tells Dad. "You understand what I'm saying?"

The woman is still staring.

Dad nods. And nods again. "Yes, I do, officer. Thank you, officer."

And then, thank God, the cop leaves.

Chris drops my hand and runs to Dad. "Are we going to jail, Dad? Kira said it's gonna be okay." He's about to cry.

My ears have been floating for a while. Now I'm suddenly so angry I can hardly see. Not that it matters. I don't want to see Dad's face anyway. "You can stop staring now!" I scream at the woman. "Show's over!" I stomp to the trash can and dump the scarf.

"Kira, don't!" Chris yells. "Dad, what is she doing?"

"Dad, get it!" Charlie wails.

Like I really need them to cry now.

"It's okay, guys." Dad walks to the can and fishes out the scarf. "See, here it is," he says, shaking out the feathers. "See. It's cool. I got it back. It's fine. We can wash it when we get home." He comes over and touches my arm. "I'll wash it, Kira, if you want."

"What makes you think I even want it?" I shout. "And it's not my home, okay? It's yours. I live in Claryville, with Grandma." I try not to look at Chris and Charlie, try not to think about what happens to them if I leave, try to stay mad enough so I can call Grandma to get me out of here.

Then it hits me: I don't need Grandma. I can

jump on the first subway that comes along, take it to Penn Station, and get out of here myself. I've got the return ticket in my wallet—the one Dad still hasn't paid me for. I turn my back on them, fold my arms, and, my heart banging, wait for the train.

The 9 rumbles in. I stand there while the people get off and push on. I stand there as—*bing-bong!*— the doors close and the train clanks out again.

I'm not going anywhere. I think I've known that for a while. My heart banging even harder, I walk back over to them.

"But, Dad?" I take a deep breath, hoping it will make my voice stop shaking. "When I said 'show's over' I meant *show's over*. I'm done. I'm not singing down here again. Ever." I take Chris and Charlie's hands. "And they're not, either. And if you want me to stay with you, neither are you. You're getting a job," I tell him. "And that's even if I don't stay. And I'm not talking about, like, music gigs, Dad, or playing in bars. I mean a real job. With a paycheck. Where people won't talk to you like you're dirt." We're on the street now, walking home. Dad's got Chris and the shopping cart with the equipment. I'm pushing the stroller, pushing it so fast they can hardly keep up with me. "And if I do stay, Dad, we're gonna have to find a school." That about-to-step-backward-off-the-diving-board feeling comes over me at the word "school." I fight it down. "And I'll need my things, which means I either have to go back home, or Grandma has to come down. So we have to talk to her. Like, right now. And the apartment's a pig pen again, and we're out of food, and if I'm going to stay here, I can't keep sleeping on the sofa. And, Dad, listen to me: I don't want anyone to hear about this. Ever."

"I used to drive a cab," he says.

It's the first thing he's said since we left the station. He mutters it so low I'm not sure he's even talking to me. I slow down a little.

"A lot of musicians drive cabs," he says. "It wasn't bad. I did it after Chris was born. I've still got my hack license. I'm thinking if I worked nights I could take care of the boys and work on my songs during the day and be there when you get home from school."

I can almost hear Grandma's voice in my ear, saying, *The baloney out of that man could keep Boar's Head going for a year.* But I slow down enough so they can walk alongside me. As casually as I can I say, "Oh, yeah?"

"They're always looking for drivers," he says. "I could give them a call."

"You're serious?"

He stops walking. "I want you to stay, Kira. The boys want you to stay."

We walk around the corner, out of the wind. He takes out our new cell phone.

My heart bangs like crazy while we wait for Grandma to pick up.

"Listen, Ma," he says, "I've been doing some thinking." He tells her that having me here has been a wake-up call; that it's time he made a steady home for his family; that he'll check out some cab companies, and then call around and find out how to register me for school. He tells her to come down right away. He says it just like that. No weaseling around, no jokes, no baloney that I detect, and my baloney detectors are going full blast. He sounds so serious and sincere I can hardly tell it's Dad.

"So then I suppose this is good news," Grandma says when he hands the phone to me. "You'll need your school clothes. And we'll need to buy you a bunch of things. I'll get someone to cover for me the rest of today, and tomorrow. I'll stop off and cash my check, and drop the dog at Phyllis's. Then I'll pack up and be on my way. It's a good thing I've got Sunday and Monday off."

"You don't sound surprised," I say. She doesn't even sound that upset.

"Kira," she says. "Your father's been wanting you with him since the day he left Claryville. I've been thinking about this since the minute you got on the train. If he really is ready to buckle down and take care of you, and if you're telling me that's what you want, too . . ."

I check to see if he's listening. He's digging around in the stroller bag trying to find Charlie's blankie, but I can tell he is. I say it anyway: "I'm not doing this for me, Grandma."

"That's not exactly a surprise, either." The sound she makes is not a laugh; I'm not sure what it is. "Listen to me, Kira. This was never meant to be a long-term arrangement, your living up here. We just kept forgetting that, you and me." She goes into a whole thing about how she'd have more of an argument if she were my legal guardian, how she's no spring chicken, how much easier it'd be for me if she weren't always working, and if we lived closer to town. It sounds too much like a speech. I'm having a hard time listening. Plus, Charlie's crying. Dad can't find Blankie.

"He's probably sitting on it," I tell Dad. He is. Dad reaches under him and pulls it out. Charlie shoves it in his mouth. Dad looks at me gratefully.

She's still talking. "And it's three years till you can get your driver's license, and you're going to need a good singing teacher and who knows what all else that I don't even know about and can't afford. And God knows your school is no great shakes, and not just the music program."

"So then you're glad I'm doing this?" I say.

She makes that snorting sound again. "I didn't say that," she says. "And don't worry, Kira. If it don't smell right to me when I get there, it ain't gonna happen."

The F Word

Jake is hurrying to fourth period Friday morning when a hand clamps down on his shoulder. "What's up?" he says, figuring it's Eugene.

Ms. Mintzer falls into step beside him. His throat seizes.

"I waited for you yesterday," she says. "Jake, I was hoping we could talk."

With anyone else he'd think that was a joke.

"I know you like to read, Jake," she says. "And you're a wonderful writer. You have no problem writing."

He waits for what he knows is coming.

"Jake, darling," she says. "You're not the only one who stutters. There are a lot of famous stutterers. Marilyn Monroe stuttered. Winston Churchill stuttered. James Earl Jones stuttered. Moses himself stuttered. A while back there was even a very successful singer who called his group the Stutterettes."

Jake's heard the famous-stutterers-throughout-the-ages speech. He knows the speech-therapy-can-do-wonders routine by heart. It's a lie. He met the school speech therapist when he first started at this school last year. He didn't like her.

"Jake," she says. "There are things you can do about your stuttering. . . ."

Yes. Get away from you. He's surprised she still calls him Jake. She might as well call him Clam Boy. Or Mr. Glitch.

"You're in a foul mood," Eugene says at lunch.

"You noticed," Jake says. They're at their usual table, but they haven't got it to themselves today. There are five kids at the end. Jake knows one of them, Cassandra, from his art class. The others must be from one of the other schools in the building. Jake's glad to see that they're ignoring him.

"You're still pissed?" Eugene asks.

Jake doesn't answer.

"At me?"

"At life," Jake says.

"I know what you mean," Eugene says. "Those three smirker guys yesterday? What jerks! And I don't care how great that singer's voice is. Her personality sucks. I mean, I was just trying to give her a friendly compliment and she looks at me, like"—

he squints down his nose and curls his lip—"'Who are *you* to talk to *me,* you prepubescent little toad?'"

"People look at us like we're toads all the time," Jake says. "It doesn't seem to bother you." The sentence slides out glitchlessly, the *B* included. He hacks at his lunch with the little plastic knife. "Filet of steel-belted radial." Glitchless again.

"Have some of this with it." Eugene's always trying to make school lunch more interesting. Today he's brought some kimchi from the salad bar at his parents' store. He pulls out a piece. "It can only help," he says. "Plus"—he gives Jake a sidewise look—"my mom says hot pepper improves the disposition. And Jake, my friend, your disposition—"

"Eeeooo, Eu*geeene*!" Cassandra stands up, fanning the air and wrinkling her nose. "What is that *smell*? Get that out of here! It smells like cabbage!"

"Because it *is* cabbage," Eugene says. "Pickled cabbage. It tastes way better than it smells. Here you go. Try some." He gets up and flaps a piece of cabbage at her, dripping juice on the table.

"Eeeooo! Don't come any closer!" she squeals.

"That kimchi stuff smells nasty," a boy with them says.

"I can smell it from here," a girl calls from the next table.

"Yo. Kimchi boy. That's why your name is Kim?" the boy says. "They named the food after you?"

"You should eat normal food," Cassandra says. "Not Chinese food. How do you expect people to eat with that stink?"

Then move! Jake wants to say. *And it's not Chinese, you moron. It's Korean.* Except that's got a *Ch* and a *K*.

He snags the piece of kimchi, holding it between his thumb and forefinger, walks over, and drops it on Cassandra's foot. "Oops," he says, looking at the wet, red chunk of cabbage lying on her white sneaker. "I'm terribly sorry." It comes out perfectly.

Cassandra screams and curses. The boys laugh.

"Uh, let me get that for you," Eugene says, grabbing a napkin and kneeling by her foot.

"Get offa me!" she says through clenched teeth as he plucks the cabbage up with his napkin. Her shoe's got a big red garlicky stain on it.

Eugene wipes at it. "See, it's fine now. All gone. Good as new."

"You're gonna have to buy me a new pair of shoes," Cassandra tells Jake. "I'm gonna have to throw these away."

"Shut up, Cassandra," another girl says. "Those shoes already smelled."

"Not like cabbage!" she screams. "Not like garlic!"

Mr. Silverman, the lunchroom monitor, trudges over, groaning. "Now what?"

Eugene tries to make his face serious. "Uh, we seem to have had a small accident, but it's under control." He pulls his asthma inhaler out of his pocket.

At first Jake is afraid Eugene's having an attack. Then he thinks, no, he's going to fake an asthma attack. Instead Eugene aims the inhaler at Cassandra's shoe as if it's some kind of special shoe cleaner or air freshener. "This will fix it right up," he says.

"Stop!" Cassandra shrieks, jumping back.

Mr. Silverman shakes his head. "I don't even want to hear it," he says before Eugene can say anything. "You two," he says, pointing a finger at Jake, who's trying desperately not to laugh, and Eugene, who's looking goofy and innocent, "take your lunches and get out of here. I don't want to see you for a week. And you"—he nods to Cassandra and her friends—"party's over. Sit down and eat your lunch."

"You better stay away from me!" Cassandra yells as they leave. "I mean it, Jake."

"So, I guess we'll be eating in the library for a while," Jake tells Eugene as they walk down the hall with their plastic trays. "That or the supply closet."

"Do you care?"

"No."

Eugene grins at him. "Me neither."

"Yeah! Freedom's just another word for nothing left to lose,'" Jake sings perfectly as they walk past another of those YOU KNOW YOU WANT TO SING. JOIN THE CHORUS signs. "'Is there a singer inside you trying to get out?'" he reads off the sign. Again, perfectly.

"I seriously doubt it," Eugene says, shaking out a fistful of Nik Naks and passing him a few. "But if there is, we'll make absolutely sure he can't."

"And why is that?" a voice behind them says.

Jake almost bolts, even though it's not Ms. Mintzer's Brooklyn accent. It's the Voice of God again. It's Ms. Hill, the music teacher. The woman who scolded Eugene in the subway.

Eugene's face is purple.

"My alto section could use some boys," she says.

"Uh, I don't think that would be us," Eugene says. "We're nonjoiners. Trust me. This works for everyone."

"You never know," she tells him. "You might surprise yourself." She turns to Jake and gives him a smile so intense he wants to look away. "What's your name?"

Occasionally, if he times it right, if he starts his "Jake" right as Eugene's finishing his "Kim," he can get it out. But not with someone staring at his mouth.

Eugene jumps in for Jake. "Uh, I'm Eugene. He's Jake."

"You should give chorus a try, Eugene and Jake," she says. "I think you'd like it. It's just too bad you eat fifth period," she says, eyeing their lunches. "We meet during sixth period lunch. But this spring, when you're planning next year's schedule, choosing your electives, think of chorus."

"Think of changing schools," Eugene says as soon as she's gone. "You know what they call her, right? Ms. Hell. Ms. Hell on Wheels. She might *look* nice . . ."

"I don't know." Jake can't get over the warmth of her smile. "I'll t-t-t-take her over M-M-M—"

"The Mighty Mintzmobile," Eugene finishes for him. "So. What's the plan today? You staying at school or leaving?"

Jake's stomach knots at the thought of cutting again. But it clenches even worse when he thinks about English. "Will you c-c-c-come with me?" he asks, even though he knows Eugene won't.

Eugene looks embarrassed. "I've got a Spanish quiz. But say hi to Cleo for me."

The first time, all he felt was fear. This time, mixed with the fear is the purest happiness. "Freedom's just another word for nothing left to lose," he sings as he walks down the street. He wonders if Ms. Hill heard him singing. If that could be why she smiled liked that. "You know, I like to sing too," he thinks of telling Cleo. It's only seven words. Five, if he drops the "you know." Though he likes the sentence better with it; the "you know" makes him sound more relaxed, laid-back.

Yeah, right, he mocks himself. In your dreams, Mr. Glitch. But he can't help practicing it both ways as he hurries to the subway station. He tries out several other variations too. Just in case.

With one last glance over his shoulder to make sure no one's seen him, he walks down the subway stairs.

And then—and he can't tell if he's relieved and thankful, or disappointed—they're not there.

"If Something Feels Too Good to Be True, It Probably Is"

"No more Subway Girl, Dad! If I'm doing this, I'm going to be a regular person in a regular family! Not Subway Girl! No singing and no subways! Not even to catch a train! I'll take the bus to school. I'll walk. . . ."

The high from reading him the riot act wore off as soon as we got back to the apartment. But it's shout or freak, so I keep shouting. "That's right, Dad." I crush up an old pizza box and cram it in the trash. I stuff the feather thing in a drawer. I shove the sofa bed closed. "Kira Stickles stays aboveground!" I yank the sheet off the easy chair and shake the crumbs onto the floor. "And no singing aboveground, either, in case you were thinking . . ." I have no clue what he's thinking. He hasn't said a word since I put the boys down for a nap. "Dad?"

He's hunched over the phone book trying to figure out who you call to find a school.

"And why are you looking for schools before you've got the job?" I yell as I hunt for the dustpan. Do we even have a dustpan? Grandma will be here any time now. The way this place looks, she'll take one step inside and run out screaming. "What *about* the job, Dad? You *are* gonna call those taxi guys, right? And how are you planning to explain to Grandma . . . ?"

I run to his room, pull the puffy periwinkle parka out of his closet, and hang it by the front door. She'll kill me if she finds out all I've been wearing is Dad's denim jacket. There's nothing to do about the ditched snow boots, though, except pray it doesn't snow. "What exactly are you going to say we've been doing for the past eight days? Or are you leaving that to me too? Dad?" A cockroach scuttles out from under the radiator and walks past his foot. I whack it with the broom. It keeps walking. "Dad!" He doesn't look up. "Dad! Have you heard a word I said?"

"Yeah," he says, circling a phone number. "No subways. You've made that kind of clear. And would you turn that TV off!"

I liked this a lot better when he was all sincere and serious and sorry. I should have known it couldn't last.

"And I'm staying here exactly *why,* again?" I yell as he takes the phone book and phone into his room to get away from me.

I follow him down the hall and sink onto the

floor outside the boys' room. I can hear Charlie talking to himself in his action-figure voice: "You're toast, Pajama Pants. Oh, yeah? Yeah! We're not afraid of you! My sister said."

Their sister feels like curling up in a ball.

Except Dad's talking too, now. I slide over and put my ear to his door. "Hey. Howya doin'? Good afternoon. Can you tell me how I go about finding a middle school for my daughter? A good one? With a good music teacher? . . . Okay, then can you tell me who I can call? Not downtown. No. West Side. We got transportation issues. . . . Yeah, right away. Yeah, fine. Give me the number. Hello? Yeah. Good afternoon, ma'am. I'm looking . . ."

"And no peeing in the bed, either, you hear me, G.I. Joe?" Charlie growls. "She doesn't like it, and she's way tougher than you."

Tough. Right. I remind myself of everything I won't miss back home, like freezing to death at the bus stop at ten to seven every morning, and then feeling carsick for an hour; health ed.; Ms. Briggs; Mr. De Marco, who sent the note home about my quote unquote *attitude*; Ms. Cramer, who's never noticed that I sleep through social studies every day. I go down the list of kids I don't like, and who don't like me. I remind myself that even my two best friends have started to seem like people from another planet. Or another life.

Tough. That's me.

When the doorbell rings I have the sudden wild thought that it's my mom, and she's not in California or wherever. She's in the city. She's called Grandma, looking for me. Grandma's told her where I am. She's here to tell Dad she made a horrible mistake, leaving us. She's come to get me out of here.

"Grandma!" The boys are out of bed and racing for the door.

I jump up and run after them.

And there she is, in her good coat and hat and her dress boots, holding the flowered suitcase and a shopping bag, giving the trash barrels and ironing board and rusty birdcage in the entryway the old fish eye. It's weird: At home I never thought about how big she is. She looks a lot wider than I remember. She looks so not New York. She looks like such an old lady.

She smells so good to me, though. I almost cry smelling that mix of wool hat and cigarettes and Pine Manor soap.

"Well," she says after she's pried me off her neck and given each boy a hug and come inside. "I was expecting worse. It's bigger than I thought. You look a little pasty, but"—she pulls Chris and Charlie to her again—"the boys seem fine. Considering. Your dad find you a school yet?"

"Yes, I did!" Dad's coming toward us. "Indeed I did. Oh, go ahead, Ma! Hug me, too. You know you want to."

He opens his arms. They do one of those stiff back-clapping things.

"And who said Russell Stickles was a screwup?" he says over her shoulder. "Who said I can't do—"

"How about the job, Russell?" She pulls out of the hug to look at him. I see her registering: *beard and ponytail, but no earrings. Clean jeans. Shirt tucked in.* "You got a job lined up?"

"Workin' on it," he says.

"Well, don't let me stop you," she says. "I can't see lugging all Kira's things in from the pickup before you've got the job. I brought along some lasagna from the freezer. Kira and I can start heating it while you make your calls."

Then I can't help myself. I do cry. I don't even care what this school is, or where. Someone's in charge here. Someone you can count on. Someone who's not me.

Dad goes back to his room and makes the calls. And he does get the job, or so he says. He tells us he just needs to go down to the cab company on Monday to fill out the forms. Grandma seems to believe him, so I guess I do.

"So let's hear about this school, Russell," she says as she finishes scrubbing out the sink and pulls a head of lettuce and carrots and tomatoes from her shopping bag.

"Here, let me help you," he says, getting a towel to dry the dishes she's just washed. He takes out the salad bowl and the dressing and the silverware. "Boys, run and get the placemats from the cupboard."

I should be helping too, I know. I'm just standing, holding on to the back of a chair, waiting to hear.

"Turns out there's this thing in New York where they have a bunch of minischools in one middle school building," he says as he sets the table. "Each one specializes in something different. Science, math, whatever. This one's called West Side Performing Arts Academy. It's for music and dance and drama." He beams at Grandma. "Sounds good, right? It sounds perfect for her. But it's not *just* about performance," he adds as I give him a warning look. "I mean, it's called an academy, right, so it's got to have good academics. And it's walking distance, like you said, Ki. No subway. So I made an appointment to check it out nine o'clock Monday morning."

I've told him a hundred times that I'm not a performer. That I'm never performing anything again. Ever. But I'm almost okay with this, till he says where the school is. Then the horrible swarmy beetle feeling starts up. It's three blocks from the subway station. I can hear the kids already: *Hey, look. It's Subway Girl. Yo, Subway Girl! You go to school? I didn't know panhandlers went to school.*

Grandma puts the tray of lasagna on the table. I can't even imagine eating.

But then she says, "I agree, Russell. The name sounds fine. But we're not jumping into anything here sight unseen. I'm gonna need to see this place for myself."

My heart lifts. "So then you'll go there with me? Instead of Dad?" They're less likely to recognize me in the puffy periwinkle, with Grandma. She's less likely to say something embarrassing.

She helps the boys to some lasagna. "If you'd like. If you think we can find the place."

I nod. "Yeah." I have no idea how we'll find the place. The only place I know how to find is the subway. But we've got the weekend to figure it out.

"Yeah. Dad can stay here with the boys. Right, Dad?"

"Then when we get back," she tells him, "you'll go down to the taxicab company and we'll babysit." She looks over at me. "What do you say, Kira? You ready to have a seat and eat some lasagna now?"

The beetles are slowing down a little. Music and art and drama could actually be okay. I pull out my chair. The lasagna smells so much like home. And they're talking to each other. Grandma's smiling. They're not fighting. "Yeah," I say. "Why not? Sure."

And when Dad raises his beer bottle and says, "To the Stickles family!" Grandma raises her water glass, Chris and Charlie raise theirs, and we all clink.

After we're done eating, I go to the hall closet and dig out the bag with the Pine Manor Christmas candy, which up to now I haven't felt like giving Dad.

He gives me a long look as he helps himself to a chocolate. "Don't mind if I do," he says. He passes the box to Grandma, who pats her lap.

"Come sit with me," she tells the boys. "I'll show you how you tell what kind of filling each one has."

I never in a million years thought this could feel like a party, but it's starting to.

"So, Ma," Dad says as both boys scramble into

her lap. "I ever tell you about some of the celebrities I had in my cab?"

"Like who?" Chris bites into a chocolate, makes a face, and gives it to Grandma.

She pops it in her mouth. "Like who, Russell?"

"Like all sorts of people. Al Pacino, Julia Roberts, what's-his-face from Eyewitness News . . ."

She gives him her fish eye. "I don't know if I even knew before today that you drove a cab," she says. "I know you're a musician, Russell. I knew you were a magician, and a birthday party clown. I know about the sword swallowing, and the fire eating. Merdlin the Magnificent—wasn't that what you called yourself?"

"Merdlin, Dad?" I raise my eyebrow.

He shrugs. "Hey, I was sixteen. And I only worked up that act to do at Pine Manor."

"And you ate swords?" Charlie jumps up from the table and runs back with his plastic one. "Can you eat this one?"

"Sorry, honey," he says. "I'm out of the sword-eating business. I'm a regular dad now, right Kira? No more acts. On the other hand . . ." He takes another chocolate, then stands up and heads over toward his guitar. "There's no law says we can't show off a little for your grandma. Don't worry," he tells me. "No one's asking you to perform. So, Ma," he says as he brings his guitar over to the table. "You and Ki go sit on the couch. Boys, come on over here by me." He whispers something to them. They giggle. "Remember I told you I've been writing songs lately?" he tells Grandma. "This is one of them. You ready, guys?"

"What are you doing?" I ask him as they both nod. Their eyes sparkle as he plays his guitar intro.

"Woke up this morning I was feeling so blue
No one in life gives a"

—Charlie does one of his mouth pops—

"what I do.
I was down on the ground. Now it's turning
  around,
Because in walked Kira. Look out now!"

"Dad!" *At least he never tried singing that one in the subway.*

"Keep listening, Ki," he says. "We're just getting to the good part. Take it, Chris!"

And Chris starts singing: "Here comes Kira. Freckle-faced Kira. Kira with the sharp green eyes."

"Charlie's turn!" Dad calls.

Grandma pokes me. "You never heard this before?"

"I been saving it for the right occasion," Dad tells her as Charlie sings in his little Charlie voice: "Here comes Kiki, True blue Kiki. Kiki with the sharp green . . . nose! Look out now! Here comes Kiki—" He peeks at me again, makes sure Grandma's watching, and sings, "Kiki with the sharp green peas!"

"He's gonna be trouble, that one," Grandma whispers to me. "Just like his dad. They're some cute kids," she says as Dad starts another verse. "And they seem to be adjusting."

You should have seen them a week ago. I don't say that.

"Oh, she's my singy dingy Kira," Chris sings. Dad's playing but he's stopped singing so he can listen. "My scarfy darfy Kira. My cutey beauty Kira . . ."

Grandma claps. "Good job, Chris!"

"I made that up," he says proudly.

"No! Really?" She turns to me. "He's smart, don't you think? Most kids that age can't rhyme like that."

"Now me!" Charlie plunks himself in front of us and starts dancing around. "My ding-a-lingy Kira, my rooty tooty Kira! My pee-pee deepy Kira! My tickle pickle Kira . . ." He's cracking himself up.

"I'll tickle pickle you!" I make a grab for him.

He scoots away, giggling. "My catch me datch me Kira! My Kira dira dira! My Kira with the oinky-doink eyes!"

"My meaty sweety Kira," Chris is giggling too. "My kitch me catch me Kira! My sad mad Kira—"

"Hey! Whoa! Hold it! Who're you calling sad?" I say, snatching him and tickling till he laughs as hard as Charlie. Then Charlie wiggles his way in and starts tickling me. Next thing I know I'm on the floor and both of them are on top of me, and we're rolling around, and they're laughing, and I'm laughing, and Grandma and Dad are smiling at each other, laughing. Then Dad pulls us to our feet and starts this ring-around-the-rosy thing, galloping us round and round, faster and faster. When Chris and Charlie collapse onto the couch, he grabs me by the waist and waltzes me around the room, spinning and dipping me backward, even though I'm yelling, "Dad, I can't waltz, Dad!"

"Sure you can!" He picks me up so my feet are dangling in the air and twirls me. "One, two, three . . . one, two, three . . ."

"Russell, you're gonna throw your back out,"

Grandma warns him. "You hurt yourself you won't be able to help me carry in Kira's bags."

"Nah," he says, "Don't worry, Ma. I got a strong back. I can carry a heavy load."

"Hey!" I punch him. "Who're you calling a heavy load? Dad, I'm dizzy! Put me down! Unless you want me to throw up on your foot!"

I'm still laughing, though. I haven't had fun like this since I don't know when.

"Those are some cute kids," Grandma says again later, after we've finally gotten them to bed and she and Dad have gone out for the bags, and we're lying in the dark. She laughs to herself. "Anyone else tried calling you Kiki, you'd clobber 'em."

We're in Dad's bed. Our bed till she goes home Monday. Then mine, supposedly. If he keeps his word and we trade. It's a lot nicer in here. You can't hear car doors slamming, or people shouting and carrying on in the street. The room has a door. The bed isn't all saggy and lumpy like the couch.

"Old Merdlin the Magician sure has a gift for getting people not to be mad at him," she says a minute later. I can't tell if she's talking to herself now, or to me. "I don't know how he does it. He is trying, though. I'll give him that. Even that song he wrote . . . and Performing Arts Academy. That could be good for you. It'd be nice if you met a nice group of girls who like doing the same things as you. And while we were out getting your stuff before, he mentioned that the middle school's got a fantastic chorus."

She makes it sound so possible. "Grandma?"

"What?" I get a whiff of Noxzema as she turns toward me.

I wish there were some way I could tell her what it's been like down here these past eight days. "Nothing. It's just . . . I keep thinking of that thing you always say. How if something feels too good to be true, it probably is. I mean, you think he really did drive Al Pacino and Julia Roberts in his cab? Or do you think that was baloney?"

She sighs. "Baloney, probably. Or wishful thinking. Or, who knows? It's New York City. It could even be true. Though I suppose you could say he can make up all the stories he wants, long as he's bringing home a paycheck and taking care of his kids."

"I told him he had to."

"So I hear," she says. "He said you laid it right out for him. He said I couldn't have done a better job myself. You're a piece of work, Kira Stickles, you know that?"

Her voice is so proud. I have to swallow hard before I dare ask what I've been waiting to ask all evening. "Am I doing something stupid, Grandma? I mean, I know we'll be fine till Monday. But what about after that? After you leave?"

She puts her arm around me. "I wish I knew, honey. You're due for something good to happen, God knows. Past due, if you ask me. Them little brothers of yours too. But I hate to say it . . . I wouldn't be rushing to give me back my horseshoe necklace if I was you."

JAKE

CHAPTER 9

Speaking Dirkish

*B*eep. "Hi, this is Ruth Mintzer, Jake's English teacher. I hope I'm not calling too early. I thought Saturday morning might be a good time to reach you. Jake and I started to chat yesterday in the hall, but he dashed off before I could finish, and then he wasn't in sixth-period class, and I have to tell you, I'm starting to get a little concerned, not only about his absenteeism, because this was his second unexcused absence this week, but also he's consistently turning his work in late, and we're not talking one day late here. I'm talking about—"

Beep. "Message has been erased."

It's pure luck that his parents were eating breakfast when she called. But Jake has a bad feeling as he and his dad set out for their run later that morning. Every corner they come to, every store or restaurant they pass, he's braced for Ms. Mintzer to pop out and nab him.

But it's not Mintzer he sees. It's the girl from the

subway. He and his dad are in the center island of Broadway, jogging in place waiting for the light to change, when he spots her on the corner. At first he isn't sure it's Cleo. She's got on a ski hat and a puffy purplish jacket, and she's not with her father and the boys. She's with a really fat woman, and they're holding hands. It's Cleo, though. There's no mistaking her face, or the way she manages to look cool even holding hands with her mom. Or maybe, Jake thinks, it's her grandmother; she's wearing an old-lady hat and clutching one of those big, old-lady pocketbooks. She's eyeing the traffic as if any second a bus might come up on the sidewalk and mow them down. Jake watches as she drops Cleo's hand, puts on her glasses, and pulls a paper from her bag. She unfolds it, reads it over, then peers up and down the street again. She says something to Cleo.

Jake wonders if they're lost.

The light changes. The girl looks across. She recognizes him. Her eyes light up. She's glad to see him! *We could wait here till they cross, and say hi,* he thinks. *We could find out if they need directions.*

But her smile dies so fast he can almost see her saying to herself, "Oh, right. Clam Boy." Instead of crossing toward them, she takes the paper from the old lady's hand, turns her head away, and starts reading.

It's better this way, Jake decides. He can already hear himself choking on "Dad, this is Cleo." And if they ask his name, which the grandmother looks like she would definitely do . . .

"Jake! We've got the light," his dad says. "Let's go."

They jog across. Cleo's still on the corner, barely five feet from them. Her eyes flick toward Jake and then flick away.

"Is that, uh, someone you know?" his dad asks as he and Jake jog past.

"N-N-N-Not ruh-ruh-ruh-really," Jake manages to get out. "Why?"

"The way she kept looking at you," Dad says.

"I've, y-y-y-you know, s-s-s-seen her around," Jake tells him. He wonders if Friday was their day off. *In which case they could be back in the station Monday, unless they've moved on.* Though for all he knows, they could be singing down at Fourteenth Street now, or in Brooklyn, or anywhere. *But if she is at the station near school on Monday,* he wonders, *will she smile at him? Unlikely, if he's with Eugene.* "D-D-D-Do they look lost to you?" he asks his father.

His dad Dad turns around. "They do," he says. "Want to, uh, go back and see?"

Jake shakes his head.

"How do you know her?" his dad asks as they

run east toward Central Park. "Is she from school?"

"No," Jake says. "I've just s-s-s-seen her. In the subway. She might not even g-g-g-go to school. She sings."

His dad frowns. "How *is* school, by the way, Jake?"

He can't know Mintzer called. Jake erased the message. Even so, Jake picks up his pace.

His dad catches up with him. "You, uh, haven't said too much this week. How is it being back?" He looks at Jake. "How's everything going?"

Jake wants to tell him. Not blurt it out, just casually ease into it. But he can't think of a casual way to ease open a can of worms. A can of worms is either closed or . . . he doesn't dare think. So he shrugs and says, "I don't know. You know. Okay, I guess."

There's another phone message Sunday. "Hi, this is Jake's English teacher, again. I know I left you a message yesterday, but it's important for us to talk. Jake is such a lovely boy, and he's got such a good head on his shoulders, and I'd hate for his stut—"

Jake erases it. And even though he knows it's a bad move, cutting Monday, he tells himself it's just this one time, just to see if Cleo's back. She isn't. It's the tuba guys again. So he promises himself he'll go to English for the rest of the week. But Thursdays are often presentation days, and his mother isn't buying his pitiful, "I'm not feeling too well. Can I stay home today?" so Thursday he cuts again. Friday, too, as it turns out. And Thursday and Friday the next week. And the next Tuesday.

"Ride around. Hang out," he says when Eugene asks him what he does when he leaves school. He tells himself it's because he's checking other subway stations for Cleo. He tells Eugene that. He tells Eugene it's fun, an adventure. A mission.

Eugene tells him he's an idiot.

Jake never dreams he can keep it going more than two weeks.

He's just about decided Mintzer has finally written him off—as she's written off that girl Shauna who spends the whole class drawing firespitting dragons on her arm, or the guys in the back who go to sleep two minutes into the period and don't wake up till the bell—when another phone call comes.

Eugene's over, so he gets it without asking. Even on good days, the telephone is not Jake's friend. "Hello?" Eugene says. Then, "I'm sorry, she's at work. No. Mr. Kandell's out too."

It sounds normal enough. Jake doesn't even look up from his math.

Today he went to English, so for a change he's not thinking about Mintzer. It's not till he hears Eugene say, "No, unfortunately he doesn't seem to be available. No. I'm his friend," that Jake's blood runs cold.

"Yeah, sure," Eugene says. "Yes. Don't worry. I guarantee he'll get it."

There's a long silence.

"What?" he asks when, after what feels like forever, Eugene hangs up.

"You're screwed," Eugene says.

CHAPTER 10

"Three o'clock tomorrow, Jake!" His mom's so angry her voice is shaking. "Ms. Mintzer's room, not the principal's office! And that's only because she likes you!" Her purse is still on her shoulder. She still has her coat on. She hasn't even taken off her snowy boots. She marched in with his dad, pulled Jake's headphones off his ears, clicked off his stereo, and laced into him. "What is going on here, Jake? What were you thinking? Where has all this running away gotten you? You've turned what could have been a molehill into a big, miserable, messy mountain. You've let this whole thing mushroom."

Part of him is glad it's over. Free as he feels each time he walks out after fifth period, it's been a strain worrying if he'll be able to sneak back in for seventh and eighth; rushing home to get to the mailbox before his dad in case Ms. Mintzer's sent a note; erasing more phone messages; lying in bed preparing for the meeting he knows has to happen, planning that if his dad says X, he says Y; if his mom says this, he says that; if Mintzer says speech therapy, he says, *I don't think so.*

The other part of him wishes he could jump up and run right now.

"She's the mushroom, Mom. A poison mushroom. A b-b-b-big, f-f-f-fat, f-f-f-fungal p-p-p-protuberance poisoning my life."

"Only because you've let it get to this."

"Well, she's not helping. She's making it worse!"

"It's not her, Jake! Ms. Mintzer is not the problem. She knows you're not comfortable speaking. Sit up, Jake! Look at me. She understands you have a problem."

Which is exactly why I have one with her. He doesn't say that. He doesn't say, *How can you expect me to be normal around her when all she sees is Mr. Glitch? And stop saying "problem"!*

He looks over at his dad for help. His dad stands there in the doorway with his lips tight and his eyes sad and disappointed. And disgusted—much worse than his mom's shouting. Which shows no signs of stopping.

"She's concerned about you, Jake! She told me even when your body's there, your mind's off somewhere!"

"Off s-s-s-somewhere?" *If only.*

"She likes your work, Jake. When you hand it in. She said you have a real way with words!"

The unfair preposterousness of it makes Jake want to cry. He turns his face to the wall, waits for them to leave, and prays for a blizzard.

There's no blizzard, but, astoundingly, there are a few flakes when he wakes up the next morning. By the time he meets Eugene, it's snowing steadily. By third period it's coming down so hard you can barely see across the street. And then, *lo and behold,* at the end of fourth period the announcement booms over the intercom: "Attention everyone. Due to the weather, school will be closing after fifth period. All regularly scheduled after-school activities are canceled."

"Where to, my liege?" Eugene shouts as he and Jake join the hordes of kids swarming through the doors and down the street. "McDonald's? Cyber Games? The comic store? Your house to get the sled?"

"Anywhere!" Jake sniffs in a deep, stinging breath. It feels like the first time he's breathed since yesterday. It feels like a miracle.

The snow's up past their shins already. They scuff through to the corner and turn onto a side street, away from the shrieking, laughing, snow-kicking, snowball-throwing crowd.

Jake pulls his hood up. A load of snow dumps down his neck.

"That's it, Eugene! Prepare to die!" Jake is reaching for a handful to throw back at him when he spots a cat carrier, like the one they use to take Leona to the vet, on top of a pile of trash bags. It's moving. He walks over and peers through the wire front. A duck looks back at him.

"Duck, as in Donald?" Eugene says, coming over for a peek. "Someone chucked their duck?"

"Looks like it." Jake squats down next to it.

The duck eyes him nervously.

"It's okay," Jake tells it. "We're not gonna hurt you. You're gonna be—"

"Uh, Jake?" Eugene taps him on the shoulder. "Forget the duck. You'll never guess who's coming!"

Jake's stomach jumps. "Mintzer?"

"No," Eugene says. "It's the girl from the subway. It's Cleo. Check it out."

And there she is, coming down the street alone, in the same denim jacket she wore in the subway and a backpack, her hair all full of snow, her shoulders hunched against the wind. She hasn't seen them.

"Ahoy, there," Eugene calls to her. "Is this by any chance your duck?"

"Excuse me?" She stops walking.

"There's a duck in it." Eugene points to the carrier.

"A live duck?" she says, still wary but coming closer. Jake can't tell if she remembers them. She holds her hair out of her eyes, leans over, and peers in the carrier. Her face is so close Jake can count the snowflakes on her eyelashes. "What's it doing out here? What are you gonna do with it?"

"Do with it?" Eugene says.

"Do with it," she says, giving Eugene the same look she gave him in the subway.

Jake needs to decide if he dares try to answer, and, if so, what to try. *Not a clue* won't do. *Bring it to the police precinct* has a *B* and two *P*s. *Call Dad* is short enough to work, but what kind of dork would say that?

"You're not gonna leave it here," she says.

"We could take it to the Bronx Zoo," Eugene says.

She gives him that same look again.

"Or we could call nine-one-one." Eugene picks up a pretend phone. "Hello. We have a duck emergency here. I'd like to report an abandoned duck. Or maybe it's not abandoned," he adds when she doesn't laugh. "This could be a ducknapping. Or a drug drop. This duck could be sitting on a stash of drugs. Or money."

She peers in the carrier again. "This duck is

freezing. It's too cold for it in that cage. It could have been in there for hours."

She's right. Jake unlatches the door.

"What are you doing?" Eugene says. "We don't know this duck. It could be vicious. It could have rabies. It could be a vampire duck."

"Ducks don't have teeth," she tells him. "You want some help?" she asks Jake. She crouches down, reaches into the carrier, pulls out the duck, and hands it to him.

It's bigger than it looked, but lighter than Leona, and more limp than vicious. It's trembling. Jake wraps his arms around it and cradles it against his chest. It lets him.

"Okay, so it's not an attack duck," Eugene says, cautiously stepping closer. "You think it's all right? It's not quacking."

"He's too cold to quack," she says. "Look at him. He's half frozen." She strokes its feathers. "See how tame he is? He's someone's pet. Somebody bought their kids a fuzzy Easter duckling and now he's not cute and fuzzy, so they threw him away."

"Why now, though?" Eugene says. "This duck hasn't been cute and fuzzy for months. This duck is immense. It's old enough to vote."

"I don't know how people can do that," she says. "Buy an animal and then just . . ."

"It's a good thing we came along," Jake tells the duck. "We'll get you warm. Eugene will help me with my jacket." He unzips it far enough to ease the duck inside, and wrap his arms around himself so it can't slip. He can feel its heart beating.

"How're you doing in there, Ducko?" Eugene says as he pulls the zipper up. "Warm and comfy? Roasty toasty?"

"Careful!" she says. "Not so high! He has to breathe."

Eugene pulls the zipper down till the top of its head shows. "Okay. Now what?"

"Yeah," she asks Jake. "What now?"

Jake's heart gives a warning *whomp*. Then the crazy, reckless, buzzy giddiness that's been building ever since he left school spills over. "Take him home," he says.

Her eyes brighten. "Can you do that?"

"Why not?" he says, even as all the reasons why not pop into his head.

"I don't know." Eugene sounds dubious. "Do they allow poultry on the subway?"

"We'll walk," Jake says, risking another sentence.

"I guess we'll walk," Eugene tells her. Then, cooler than Jake thought possible for Eugene, he adds, "You coming with us?"

"Me?" She suddenly looks flustered. "No. I don't know. Am I? I mean, I could, I guess. If you don't live too far. My dad doesn't leave for work till after three."

And Jake knows *his* dad won't be home. "You've got time," he says. That's four sentences to human beings with no crashes!

"Onward, then," Eugene says. "The Three Ducksketeers." He picks up the empty carrier and they start walking, Jake and the duck in the middle, Eugene and Cleo on either side. They walk for a block or so without saying anything. Then Eugene says, "Not to be nosy. But don't you have to get to work too?"

"No," she says, not looking at him.

"I mean, I'm assuming you're still singing, right, even though we haven't—"

"No," she says, walking faster. "I go to school."

"Oh, yeah?" he says. "Which school?"

She hesitates a second. "Performing Arts."

"As in West Side Performing Arts?" He nods in the direction of school.

She still looks straight ahead. "Uh-huh."

"Get out!" he says, punching Jake's arm. "That's where we go! I mean, not Performing Arts. Science Center. But it's the same building. On the ground floor."

"I know," she says.

"You know it's the same building?" Eugene says. "Or you've seen us?"

She doesn't answer.

"You have seen us!" Eugene says before Jake can catch his eye or poke him. "I don't believe it! And you didn't say hi or anything? To your biggest fans? You realize we look for you in the subway every day, and not just in this station. I mean, my friend here has been—" Jake pokes him. "What I mean is"— Eugene hardly misses a beat—"have you been there this whole time, or is this something new? We knew you weren't sixteen! Right, Jake?"

Jake doesn't answer, but he wants to know as badly as Eugene does.

"So, what grade are you in?" Eugene says. "And if you're in school, when do you guys do your act?"

"You know," she says, "for someone who's not being nosy, you're pretty nosy. And you don't listen, either. I don't have an act. I told you that." She starts walking even faster.

"What did I say?" Eugene asks Jake. "Did I say something wrong? All I meant," he calls after her, "was it's too bad you *don't* have one, because then *you* could take the duck. You could put him on a little leash, or he could sit on a crate and do ducky percussion. 'Oh, a bad song is better than no song! Quack! A bad song—'"

She wheels around. "What is your problem?" Her eyes flash with anger.

"*My* problem?" Eugene looks baffled. Or hurt. Jake's not sure. Or he could be pissed. "You think because you can sing—"

"You know something?" she snaps. "I don't need this! You guys deal with the duck. I'll see you around."

"No. *You* know something?" Eugene says stiffly. "I don't really have a way with ducks. I don't even like ducks. Why doesn't she just go with you and I'll walk back over to the subway and go on home?" He hands Jake the cat carrier.

Jake searches for something light to say, something smart and funny, preferably ridiculous, like the lines Eugene's always coming up with for him. All he can think of is *Huh? What just happened? We were having so much fun. Don't do this to me, guys. You can't leave me with this duck!*

"D-D-D-Don't b-b-b-be like that," he stammers out.

He means both of them, but Eugene's the one who answers. "Yeah, well," he says. "I guess that's just me. It's what I'm like." And with a tight, "See ya," to Jake, and not a word to Cleo, he heads off.

She stays.

CHAPTER 11

*H*e was just trying to make you like him, Jake wants to explain. *Eugene gets all weird and nervous when he can't make someone laugh. But he's a great guy. Eugene's the best.* "Eugene's unique," he tells the duck.

"I hope he can breathe okay in there," she says as they start walking.

"Yeah," he says.

There's no one on the street here. The only sounds are the slosh of car tires and the scrape of a snow shovel. They're walking west now. The closer they get to the river, the fiercer the wind. He keeps expecting her to turn off, but she doesn't.

"Brrrr," she says, wrapping her arms around herself.

He looks at her in her thin denim jacket. The duck is keeping his top half warm, but his knees are tingling. His hands and feet are numb. *You could carry the duck,* he wants to say. *It's like having your own down vest.*

"What park is that?" she asks.

"R-R-R-Riverside," he manages to get out.

"Oh, right. Because it's alongside the Hudson River. Duh. And that big statue thing?"

He's pretty sure he can't say Soldiers and Sailors Monument, even to the duck, so he pretends not to hear. They're almost at his building. He's worrying about all the things he'll have to say: *Can you reach into the outer pocket of my backpack and get my key? . . . Could you please press fifteen? . . . You're gonna need to take off your shoes before you go inside. . . . Do you mind holding this duck for a second so I can get my jacket off? . . . Would you like a towel or something for your hair?* But they make it past the grinning doorman—grinning, Jake is sure, because he's with a girl—and up in the elevator and into the apartment, without his having to say a word.

But just as that dizzy, giddy, what's-gonna-happen-next feeling starts bubbling up again, he hears a weird, growling, moaning howl.

The duck scrabbles frantically, trying to get its wings open. Jake tightens his hold.

"Uh-oh," she says. "You didn't mention you had a cat."

Leona is standing in the kitchen doorway, the

hair on her back all puffed up, her ears flat, her eyes dark and glittery.

A quack comes from inside Jake's jacket.

Leona hisses, growls deep in her throat, then slowly, stealthily, menacingly, like a tiger on the nature channel, creeps toward him.

"Your cat thinks you've brought his dinner," Cleo says as the duck tries to flap its way out.

Jake runs for the bathroom.

"He's coming after you!" she calls.

Jake slams the door shut and unzips his jacket. The duck half flies, half tumbles into the tub.

"Sorry," Jake tells it as it stands up, spreads its wings, shakes out its feathers, and gives Jake a beady, red-eyed glare.

"Coast's clear!" Cleo calls through the door. "I closed your cat in a bedroom. How's the duck?"

"P-P-P-Pissed," Jake says, opening the door.

"Not half as pissed as your cat," she says, coming in.

The duck gives her the same angry glare.

"Why are you looking at me like Evil Doom Duck?" Jake tells it. "We just saved your life. Twice."

"That's how ducks always look," she says, coming closer. "He's, like, Okay, you saved me. Now how about some service?"

"What do ducks eat?" Jake asks it.

"Anything they can get," she says. "Grass, bugs, duck chow. . . ."

"C-C-C-Cat chow?" He makes the mistake of trying to say it to her, instead of to the duck. He turns away so she won't see how red his face is, takes off his jacket and drapes it over the shower stall. She's still wearing hers. Her hair, now that the snow's melted, hangs down in long, drippy curlicues. He hands her a towel.

"Thanks," she says, wiping her face and around her neck.

"I'll be right back," Jake tells the duck. He hurries to the kitchen for the box of cat chow and a container, grabs a bag of cookies from the cabinet, and the bowl of grapes from the fridge, and runs back to the bathroom.

She's standing at the sink, looking at herself in the mirror, braiding her hair.

The instant the duck spots him, it lets out a loud quack.

She jumps.

"S-S-S-Sorry," Jake says as he sets the food down on the counter. The duck quacks eagerly.

"Meow Mix," he tells it.

"That should work," she says. "And ducks love

vegetables, so they'll probably eat fruit. But"—she eyes the cookies—"those look kind of good to give to a duck, don't you think?"

"They aren't for you," he tells it. "The grapes, either." He opens the cookie bag and holds it out for her.

"Ooh!" she says, reaching in.

Jake takes one too. The duck's eyes follow the cookies to their mouths.

"You better watch out," she tells him as the duck quacks again. "Ducks are bold. He's liable to fly up and snatch it. The neighbors' ducks used to walk down the road and come up on our porch and eat our dog's food right out of his bowl."

Can ducks fly? he wants to ask her. *And where are you from, anyway, that you know all this?* Instead, he pulls out a few pieces of cat chow and crouches beside the tub.

The duck's head darts out.

"Hey! Ow!" Jake shouts, shaking his hand, even though it's more of a pinch than a bite.

She giggles. "I told you they were bold. That's not how you do it. You have to hold your hand flat. Like this." She holds her palm out. "Good thing they don't have teeth, right?" She kneels next to him and shakes a few pellets onto her palm. "See," she says as the duck dips its head and delicately nibbles them.

Jake puts the food on the floor between them and holds out his palm. The duck's bill tickles him. He laughs.

They take turns feeding it. Each time they stop to eat something, it opens its wings and quacks. Not just one quack, but a loud *Waaack, wack, wack, wack, wack, wack!*

"The neighbors' ducks?" she says. "They also eat Chef Boyardee, if you can believe that. SpaghettiOs. Is this your only bathroom?" She looks in the tub, which is already gross.

"Unfortunately, yes," Jake tells the duck.

"That could be a problem," she says. "I mean, unless your mom and dad are really, *really* nice. Or don't like baths. Or unless you can, like, rig up some kind of duck diaper, like with a plastic bag."

Jake makes a face.

She giggles again. "We should probably have put down some newspaper or something before we put him in. Too late now, I guess."

They take turns feeding it until she says, "I wonder if Meow Mix is bad for ducks."

"Now she asks us."

She giggles harder. Jake can hardly believe all

this. Part of him can't wait to tell Eugene. Another part wants to keep it his secret.

"You know what I bet happened?" she says as he fills the empty grape bowl with cold water from the tap. "Some couple had a fight, and the wife packed up and left, and the man was so upset he put the duck out with the garbage. Unless it was . . . oh, wow!" She nods toward the duck, who, now that it's finished drinking, is gazing up at them. "Look! No more Evil Doom Duck. He likes you. You're his new mommy. Or daddy."

Jake reaches out his hand and strokes its head, coming at it from behind so he won't get nipped. The duck lets him.

"Yeah," he says. Now that it's stopped glaring, it's kind of good-looking. It has a nice neck and sleek white feathers and cool orange feet. "Yeah," he says. "I'm . . . g-g-g-good with animals." Then he adds, "So are you."

"Tell that to your cat," she says, holding out her hand. There are two deep tooth holes on it. She makes a sheepish face. "He bit me. When I grabbed him up before."

"I should have warned her," he tells the duck, stroking it again. "My cat bites everyone. Except me." He doesn't dare look at Cleo as he says to her,

"You could have c-c-c-calmed her down. It's easy. You just have to . . . s-s-s-sing to her. That's what I always d-d-d-do. She l-l-l-loves it."

"I should go," she says. She stands up and puts the grape stems in the waste basket. "Now that the duck's happy, and I've eaten all your food."

"We're leaving now," he tells the duck. "Don't go flying around the room or anything." Then he gets up too, and they go to the living room.

There are two wide windows facing out toward the river. On a clear day you can see all the way up to the bridge and across to New Jersey. "It must be so nice living so high up like this," she says, walking over to them and looking out, though there's nothing to see now but swirling snow. "I bet you get great sunsets."

Why, Jake's wonders, *did he tell her he sang?* He doesn't sing. She sings. *And considering how upset she got when Eugene brought it up, she doesn't want to hear about that, either.*

"So, what are your mom and dad gonna say?" she says, still looking out the window. "They'll be pissed, right? I mean a duck isn't exactly a city pet. And that's a nice bathroom. And this is a pretty beautiful apartment." She walks to the fireplace and studies the photos of Jake's parents on the mantel. "They look very nice. They look like they might not

totally hate ducks." She walks over to the piano.
"W. A. Mozart" she reads off the music book open
on the piano stand. "Sonatas. It must be cool to
have a piano. This one is beautiful. Is it a grand?"

Jake can see she's dying to try it. "Go ahead."

"I can't really play," she says, but she pulls out
the piano bench and sits down. He comes over
behind her. "Do you play?" she says as she starts in
on "Chopsticks."

"No," he says. It's simpler than explaining that
he took lessons for three years. "My dad does."

"This man back home?" she says, still playing.
"Mr. Corrigan? He said he'd teach me, but this is as
far as we got with it. This and 'Heart and Soul.' You
play any other instrument?"

"No. I'm just a"—he wants to say *music lover*—
"l-l-l-listener."

She starts another variation. "You sing, though."

"Uh-uh." He wants to add: *But I have a headful of
songs all the time. I know the words to everything—
songs I love, songs I don't like, even songs I hate.*
"Uh-uh," he says again.

"You said you did," she says. "You said your cat
thinks you're talented."

He's glad he's standing behind her so she can't
see his face.

"I was just thinking you might be in the chorus," she says. "You know. At school." She plays a few more measures. "I thought about doing it. But I don't know. I'm not singing anymore. I quit singing. In case you didn't notice." She stops playing and pushes back the piano bench and makes a face. "And what am I still doing here, right? I said I was going, and then I didn't go."

"You don't have to."

"Yeah, I do," she says. "I don't want to make my dad late for work."

He follows her to the foyer. She sits on the bench and puts on her wet sneakers. "Those cookies were good," she says. "So were the grapes." She stands up and puts on the backpack. "Let me know what happens with the duck. Just don't name him. You give him a name and your parents decide to cook him for supper or something, you'll be all upset. Oh, and by the way," she says, busying herself with her buttons. "Speaking of names? Mine's not Cleo. It's Kira."

"Hi!" It pops out before he can think better of it. "I'm . . ."

"Jake," she says, nodding. "I know."

He's so overjoyed that she said it for him and that she hasn't noticed how ridiculous it is saying "hi" to someone on her way out the door that the rest slides out almost glitchlessly: "I'm, uh, I'm glad you came."

"Yeah," she says, still not totally meeting his eyes, but smiling, nodding, then nodding again. "Hi."

CHAPTER 12

"A duck? Are you out of your mind?" Jake's mom shouts before she even sees it. "I am not having a duck in my bathroom! You've got enough problems on your plate without adding a duck!"

His dad's nodding, tight-lipped. "The duck's out of here!" he says. "Start looking for another home for it. Right now!"

Except for dinner, and a few quick duck visits—the duck greets him each time with eager quacks and eats delicately from his hand; but his mom is right, their bathroom would disgust even a diehard duck lover—Jake spends the rest of the evening on his bed with his headphones on. He knows he should be doing a search for animal adoption agencies, planning what to say to them. But just the thought of talking on the phone, even to Eugene, ties his vocal cords in knots.

Maybe I can get Eugene to make the duck calls, he thinks as he paces up and down the subway platform the next morning. *Maybe I can get Eugene to come to the Mintzer meeting with me too, while he's at it.* Because that was his dad's last message to him as he left the house: "Reschedule it, Jake. Today. Putting it off won't make it any easier."

At one end of the platform an old big-bellied man sings with a guitar: "*Bésame, bésame mucho.*" Most subway performers are real musicians. This man hasn't even bothered to tune his guitar. His voice is off-pitch. Jake wonders where he finds the nerve to get up in front of the world and moo like that. Even so, when Jake's train roars in, he lets the doors open and close, and stands there, watching him. *The duck is a better singer than this guy is,* he tells himself as yet another train comes and goes. *I sing better than he does. Eugene sings better.*

That's when the idea comes to him. It's not the idea he was looking for. It does nothing for his duck problem. It's complicated, and convoluted, and crazy, and wild, and risky, and probably stupid. It could also be the best idea he's ever had.

"I just figured out what to do about the Mintzmobile!" he tells Eugene the instant he sees him. "We're joining chorus! Remember when we met Ms. Hill in the hall and she said chorus meets during sixth period lunch and we should switch our lunch periods next year so we can be in chorus? Well, why wait? If we switch lunch to sixth right now, I'll have to switch English! Hello, Hill! Bye-bye Mintzer! And you hate Mr. Silverman, so it works for you, too! And you had all those violin lessons, right, so you can read music!"

"Whoa. Slow down, Jake!" Eugene says as Jake lays it out for him, runs through the schedule changes and permissions they'll each need. "Jake! Chill! You're scaring me." They're at their usual spot in front of the bodega across from the school yard, away from the crowds. He holds out his bag. "Have a bagel. Eat some Nik Naks."

"N-N-N-No! L-L-L-Listen t-t-t-to me!" Jake's so excited he can hardly breathe. "We can do this. I can be in your English class. With Estrada. Why didn't I think of this b-b-b-before? C-C-C-Come on, Eugene. It's b-b-b-brilliant!"

"Yes." Eugene unwraps his bagel, opens the two halves, scrapes off the excess cream cheese with a coffee stirrer, then wipes it onto his napkin. "It's brilliant. But there's a problem. Even if everyone says yes, if we join chorus, we have to be in chorus."

Exactly. And no one talks in chorus. In chorus all you do is sing. Jake doesn't say this. "We can handle that!"

"I love how you keep saying 'we'!" Eugene says.

Jake doesn't answer. He's just seen Kira crossing the street, walking past the knot of kids on the corner without even a glance, walking straight toward them. His heart bounces. Till he remembers that she and Eugene hate each other. And that he still hasn't told Eugene any of what happened with her yesterday.

"Hey," Kira says to Jake. She eyes Eugene. He eyes her back. "What's up?"

Eugene wipes his mouth and squares his shoulders. "Not much," he says finally. "Jake's trying to talk me into joining chorus. What a bad idea that is, right?"

Kira turns to Jake. "Seriously?"

She clearly thinks he is serious.

Is he? It was one thing to dream up this plan, or think it was brilliant, or even tell it to Eugene, who's hated it enough to keep Jake from freaking. *But actually do it?* Jake can see the part where he saunters past Ms. Mintzer's door. He can almost see himself and Eugene walking into the auditorium. But when he tries to imagine what chorus might be like . . .

They're waiting for him to say something.

"Uh . . . D-D-D-Dirk says h-h-h-hi," he says eventually.

Eugene looks at him. "And Dirk would be . . . ?"

A wave of joy and relief washes over him. He's changed the subject. He grabs the bagel from Eugene's hand and takes a bite. "The duck."

"So then I guess they didn't eat him," Kira says. "Does that mean he can stay?"

Jake shakes his head.

"So then what's gonna happen?" she asks him.

"Dirk goes to the duck shelter?" Eugene says. "Duck goes to the Dirk shelter?" He looks across the street at the kids heading for the school. "We better get going," he tells Kira.

"Dirk?" he says, as soon they leave her. "You named your duck without telling me?"

"The name just p-p-p-popped into my head," Jake explains. "Like chorus!" Which is starting to seem like a serious idea again.

Eugene stops. "What is up with you? You meet some girl and—"

"She's not some girl! It's not about her! She's not even in chorus. It has n-n-n-nothing to do with her." Jake feels himself blushing. He wonders if he's lying. He knows this is the moment to say, *Oh, and, by the way, her name's not Cleo. It's Kira.* "Just once, Eugene," he says. "We'll go today and check it out. That's all I'm asking. I'm not s-s-s-saying to cut study hall. You'll get a pass from the office. I'll go with you during lunch."

"Today, you said." Eugene looks even less pleased.

They're at their entrance now. They head inside and start toward their homerooms.

Jake holds his breath.

Eugene stows the remains of his bagel in his backpack. "So then assuming I say yes to this extremely bad idea. And I get the pass. What do you do?"

His eyebrow is still up. He's still got that peevish squint. But he's going to say yes; Jake can feel it.

Jake checks up and down the hall. No sign of Ms. Mintzer.

"It will be my l-l-l-last cut," he tells Eugene as "Freedom's just another word for nothing left to lose" starts playing in his head and the tingly, buzzy, booming-in-the-ears giddiness threatens to bubble over. "I swear to God!" He puts his hand on his heart. "If we like this, I will never cut English again."

"And if we hate it?" Eugene says. "What'll you do then? Change your schedule anyway? And cut chorus?"

"Uh"—Jake makes a face—"that's what I was thinking."

But even as the words leave his mouth he pictures himself talking to his dad later, saying, *See? I wasn't running away!* Or not just running, anyway. He hears Kira saying: "You sing. Your cat thinks you're talented." And Ms. Hill, saying, with that smile of hers, "You never know. You might surprise yourself."

"Forget I said that," he tells Eugene, forcing back the other voice, the one going, *Oh, yeah, right, Clam Boy. In your dreams, Mr. Glitch.* "It was a joke," he says, and hopes to God he's not lying.

CHAPTER 13

"There are no boys here. I knew it," Eugene whispers as they slip into the last two seats on the end of the second row of the auditorium. "It's all eighth-grade girls. Except them." He nods toward a couple of shrimpy sixth-grade boys coming down the aisle.

"Huh? What?" Jake's senses are tuned so high that he can feel people's eyes on them, smell the fries a girl down the row has brought from the cafeteria, taste the egg sandwich Eugene just gulped down. When the old lady at the piano plays a chord, he jumps.

The chatting stops. The old lady begins to play a gospel rhythm.

Eugene shakes out a handful of Nik Naks. "You don't know what you're getting us into," he tells Jake. "This is without a doubt the stupidest, worst—"

"Shhh!" The girl in front of them turns and frowns as Ms. Hill enters through the door beside the stage.

"Hello. Good afternoon. How are you all today?" Ms. Hill strides back and forth, nodding, greeting people, looking into people's eyes. "I was in a testy mood before I got here. But now I'm happy, because I see not only my old friends, but a few new faces. Welcome!" She stops in front of the boys. *"Welcome!* You're the gentlemen I talked to in the hall. I'm so pleased to see you. I'm delighted you'll be singing with us. Jake and Eugene, isn't it?"

Jake nods, not breathing. If she makes them sing alone, he's dead. If he doesn't die then, he knows Eugene will kill him later.

She moves on down the row. His breath comes out in a whoosh.

Eugene looks at him. "Did you see her feet?" he whispers. "No woman has feet that big. I think she might be a man. And check out the pianist. Am I crazy or does she look like a camel?"

"Excuse me." Ms. Hill is back. "Why are you talking? You are not in my chorus to talk. And why are you sitting?" she asks everyone. "We've got work to do. Stand up, please." Sixty kids jump to their feet. "All right, now. Open your mouths wide. Drop your jaws. Get into the longness of the pitch. Ha, ha, ha, ha, ha!" she sings.

"She's laughing at us already!" Eugene whispers as everyone "ha, ha"s along with her.

"Excuse me," she says again. "Excuse me. You're not singing. You're talking. Please leave. Leave now."

"Fine with me," he mutters.

"Not you," she tells him. "I'm talking to Maya. Who knows the rules. That's right, Miss Maya. You. Please leave. Good-bye." She points to the door beside the stage, then, as the girl slinks out, turns to the group, and starts to sing: "Wade in the water . . ."

It's the first time Jake's heard her. Her voice is like velvet. Or maple syrup.

"Wade in the water, children," everyone sings after her.

He's heard the chorus, so he knew how good they were. But it's one thing hearing them from the audience. It's another thing altogether being right there, inside all that sound.

"Who's not on pitch?" Ms. Hill calls, walking up and down the row. "If you can't sing on pitch, don't sing at all. Hands down by your sides. Stop looking sad. And don't get timid on me. Sing out." She starts again. "Wade in the water . . ."

"Isn't that Letitia from the lunchroom over

there?" Eugene whispers. "The dreaded Cassandra's friend? The one who hates you?"

Jake takes a deep breath. "Speaking of hate," he whispers back, "I have something to tell you. I should have told you before we saw her this morning. Her name's not Cleo. It's Kira."

"What?" Eugene forgets to whisper.

"Excuse me." This time Ms. Hill *is* talking to them. "Is there a problem?"

Eugene throws Jake a *yes!* look, then shakes his head.

"Good. Thank you. Now . . ." She pooches her lips out, and goes *"Shrooo!"* The sound is somewhere between an opera singer and a train whistle. *"Shrooo! Shrooo!"*

The chorus "shrooo"s with her. She's still got her eye on Eugene, so he and Jake "shrooo" too, but Eugene's comes out more like *"Arooo!"* and it goes on too long.

Ms. Hill ignores him. "Squeals, now. *Eeeeeeeee!*" She starts it somewhere up near high C and lets her voice drop low.

"That I can handle," Eugene says, making a noise like a mouse being strangled.

Ms. Hill's eyes flash. "You know," she says. "I'm starting to get mad. No . . ."—she pauses and lets her voice get sweet again—"no. I'm not. And you want to know why? Because you're new, and I'm so glad you're here."

"Sorry," Eugene says. "Sorry. Sorry." He repeats it, then, as Ms. Hill glares again, clamps his hand over his mouth.

She gives him one last warning look and turns to the pianist. "Ms. Bolden, a little marching music, please. Move to the back of the auditorium, everyone. Form a line."

Ms. Bolden's march has a hip-hop beat. Ms. Hill claps along. "Let's go, people. Don't waste my time. Step . . . step!" She hums and taps and claps. "Let's go! Let's go. Keep space between you. When I say 'step,' children, *that's* when you're supposed to step. Have fun with it. Easy. Bounce. Make small steps. Good. Smaller. *No!* You're *not* on *step!* Stop looking at your feet!" She's shouting now. "You children are boring me to death. Put some life in it. Feel the beat. Sway. Bounce. Do *something.* Step! Step, step. Step! Come *on* guys. Don't be shy."

The girl ahead of Eugene has started to do a whole little dance routine. Eugene tries to imitate her. The Nik Naks in his pockets rattle. It sounds like he has twenty packs in there. Jake prays he doesn't decide to pull his arms out of his sleeves and do his windmill thing.

"Better!" Ms. Hill cries. "Now he's getting it! Very good. Yeah! Nice! Now you're having fun with it!"

And Jake is. Almost. As long as he doesn't let himself look around to see if anyone is watching.

They march around the auditorium a few times. Then Ms. Hill moves back toward the stage, claps her hands, and tells everyone to come up and get the music.

As they file to the front Jake notices a girl peering in through the door next to the stage. For an instant he thinks it might be Kira.

"Sorry I'm late," the girl says, making a face.

"No, no!" Ms. Hill says. "You're just in time. Don't sit down, Michelle. Come right up here with me. I want you to teach everyone this song. Sing the first verse through for us."

Michelle looks terrified. "All by myself?" she squeaks. "It's in Latin."

"You know it, Michelle," Ms. Hill says. "You sang it last year."

Michelle makes a face. "I'm scared."

"Scared?" Ms. Hill pretends to be shocked. "Of these guys? I don't believe that. Cheer her on, people.

Make her comfortable. Come on, now, Michelle. You can do it. You know this song perfectly."

Ms. Bolden starts the introduction. Jake can almost feel Michelle swallow, feel her heart clench up as she jams her hands in her pockets then starts to sing. Or tries. Her mouth moves, but there's no sound.

"What's that?" Ms. Hill says, cupping her hand behind her ear. She turns to the chorus. "Do you all hear anything?"

"No, Ms. Hill," everyone says.

That could so easily be him up there; Jake can hardly bear to look at Michelle.

She starts again. She has a pretty voice. It's just that it's shaking so hard.

Ms. Hill lets her sing a few measures then holds up a hand to stop her. "Okay, people," she says. "Tell me two good things Michelle did."

"She didn't die?" someone says.

A few kids snicker, but Ms. Hill says, "That's right! She's still alive. Is that true, Michelle?"

Michelle screws up her face.

"Don't make faces," Ms. Hill says. "We know you're embarrassed. We all get embarrassed. Everyone gets embarrassed. It's embarrassing being up here in front of everyone."

Eugene starts to say something. Jake pokes him to shut up.

There's a buzz of talking in the back and a few giggles. Ms. Hill frowns. "If you are talking, please leave. If you are fidgeting, please leave. Remember, this could be you up here. Let's give this child some support. What else was good?"

Someone calls out, "She knows the words."

"Yes, Tamika, she does." Ms. Hill nods.

"She's on pitch," one of the boys says.

"That's right." Ms. Hill nods again. "She's got good pitch. And how's her voice, Felipe?"

"It's good," Felipe says.

"Not 'good,'" Ms. Hill corrects him. "It's very good. Now what could she do to make it better?"

"Look up!" someone calls. "Project."

"Be brave," the other boy adds.

Ms. Hill looks at Michelle. "Are you brave enough to try again?"

Michelle makes another face, then nods and starts again.

When she's done everyone claps. Ms. Hill puts her arm around Michelle and gives her a squeeze. "Now I ask you, people," she says. "Is that a beautiful voice or what? Sing with her, everyone. See if you all can sing like that. Michelle will lead you.

Come on, Michelle. We need to hear you over them."

Ms. Bolden starts the intro. Michelle is smiling so hard that for a few bars she can't sing at all.

Jake has only heard the song this one time. He doesn't know Latin. But his mouth opens; it's moving; he's breathing; the words are flowing out, one after another, easy and glitchless. He glances over at Eugene a few times to check if he's still pissed about Kira, to see how he's doing, to see if he likes this. Then he forgets about Eugene and just sings. He can't really hear himself. His voice has disappeared inside everyone else's. It's there, though. He can feel it. And when they finish the Latin song, and Ms. Bolden starts the next song he sings that, too.

Eugene's started giving him looks, like, *Uh, Jake? A little self-restraint might be good here.* He keeps singing. Eugene was wrong. He did know what he was doing. He won't need to cut chorus. He's doing this.

CHAPTER 14

As soon as he gets out of homeroom that afternoon, he runs up to the main floor to wait for Kira. "I did it!" he says the instant she comes through the door. She's by herself again. So's he. Eugene's at the dentist. "I went!" he tells her.

"To chorus? Really?" She grins at him.

He nods.

"And you liked it?" She doesn't seem the slightest bit surprised to see him. "Did Eugene go?" she asks as they walk toward the main entrance. "Did he like it?"

Jake makes a face. "He said it was almost as much f-f-f-fun as an a-a-a-asthma attack. He said he'd rather spend f-f-f-forty-five minutes scraping k-k-k-kimchi off Cassandra's f-f-f-foot than go again." He also said he preferred an asthma attack to Kira, but Jake's not worried. He's never known Eugene to stay mad. "It's fine," he tells her. "I've got till Monday, now, to work on him." That comes out so well he eases toward the wall so they don't get trampled, and keeps going. "You should h-h-h-hear them! You should hear Ms. H-H-H- . . . sing! I mean, I thought *you* were good. I mean, you *are* . . . s-s-s-so g-g-g- . . . you're . . . I've n-n-n-never heard . . ."

He wants so badly to tell her. He knows that anyone who sings the way she does will get it.

"And Eugene k-k-k-keeps saying how h-h-h-horrible Ms. Hill is, but she w-w-w- . . . Not if you were tr-tr-tr-trying. Not with m-m-m-me! And there was this one g-g-g- . . . Sh-Sh-Sh-She was so . . . sh-sh-sh- . . ."

He's waited all afternoon to describe this to her, to tell her how exciting it felt being surrounded by voices, hearing that great old-lady piano player under them, pulling them along; to tell her how Ms. Hill made Michelle feel so good when she was so scared; how Ms. Hill's whole thing was to be brave, sing out, be serious, and work hard, but to love the music. He's got so much to say the words are stacked up ten deep in his throat.

"It's attitude, children!" he shouts finally.

Kira looks at him like he's lost it.

"I don't need wimps in my chorus!" he proclaims even more dramatically, so she'll get that it's his Ms. Hill voice. "I don't need little mice!" It's like talking to cats, or ducks. He can do everyone's voice but his own. "And why are you apologizing? You have nothing to apologize about! It's attitude I want here! Show me some attitude!"

Kira's eyes brighten. "That's what she said, really? She wants people with an attitude?"

"N-N-N-Not *a-a-a-an* attitude. A-A-A- . . . titude."

"She didn't, like, test your reading and stuff?"

"Uh-uh. She didn't even a-a-a-ask i-i-i-if . . ."

She asked nothing, except that you give yourself to the music. Let it out. And he did. Which is why he could kill his mouth for doing this to him now. He could rip it off his face for making it so hard.

"So, I guess Dirk didn't get eaten by your cat," she says after what feels like hours. "Did she try again?"

"N-N-N-Not yet."

"That's good. And he's still in the bathroom?"

"W-W-W-When I left."

"And does he still think you're his mommy?"

"Uh-huh. He also might think he's a r-r-r- . . . ooster. He started . . ."—he's doing better now, he can breathe again, but he doesn't dare try a Q— "*wacking* when it was still dark." He quacks like a champ.

She giggles. "He wanted you to go in and keep him company."

He nods. "Yeah. Every time I come in, he's, like . . ." Jake does a short, happy *Wack!* "Ex . . . c-c-c-cept if I don't have anything for him to eat. Or he doesn't like what I br-br-br- . . . Then it's . . ." He imitates the duck's disgusted *Wack!*

"I see you're learning duck talk," she says.

"D-D-D- . . . uckish," he says.

"Dirkish," she says. "You speak excellent Dirkish."

"There's also . . ." They're getting some strange looks from kids walking by. He ignores them and does a loud outraged *"Waaack!"*

"What's that one?" she says, laughing.

"You c-c-c- . . . ome near my f-f-f-food, you die!"

"I thought it was *Danger! Here come the dogs! Run for the pond!* Who'd he do it to?"

"Uh . . ." He never thought he could laugh about this. "My mom."

She giggles. "What'd she do?"

"Th-Th-Th-Threw a f-f-f-fit. Another one."

"Uh-oh!" she says.

"Oh, no," he says. "W-W-W-We're way past uh-oh, here."

She gives a quick quack under her breath. It's so soft he barely hears it. There's no mistaking it, though. It's the danger quack. It's *Head for the pond!*

"Jake Kandell?" a stern and angry voice behind him demands. "Is that you?"

He whirls around.

In some corner of his mind he knows it's absurd to be so scared of her. He knows that if this were someone else's teacher barreling toward them on her tiny feet with her giant black-frame glasses, like a Saturday-morning cartoon character, he'd be laughing. And for one nanosecond, before his throat clenches and his blood drains to his feet, he feels an insane flash of happiness that she did see him laughing. And joking around. And talking.

"You're going to have to excuse us," Ms. Mintzer tells Kira. "This young man and I are about to have a serious talk. Jake, I just this minute left another message for your mother."

Kira shoots him a quick, worried look and heads toward the door.

"Where were you today, Jake?" Ms. Mintzer demands, catching him by the arm. Jake's almost sure that's against the law. He doesn't say anything. "Why weren't you in English sixth period?" He doesn't answer. "I didn't really expect your parents to come in and meet with me on a snow day, but you could have stopped by to tell me. Instead, what do you do? You cut my class again! And then

I find you standing out here gabbing with your friend, without a care in the world. I've given you more chances than I'd give any other student, Jake, because my heart went out to you. I've bent over backward here. . . ."

She goes on lecturing, marching him down the hallway toward the office. Jake hears and doesn't hear. What he's mostly hearing is himself, doing that Ms. Hill imitation. He's not a wimp or a mouse; he knows that. He's got all kinds of attitude. But how is anyone else going to know that when he can't talk?

Ms. Mintzer's still going on about how actions have consequences and cutting class has consequences, and there are only so many cuts that can be tolerated before steps must be taken when he hears Kira's voice.

"He wasn't cutting."

Ms. Mintzer drops his arm. She stops walking. "I beg your pardon?" she says as Kira catches up with them.

Jake's heart bounces. He had no idea she was following them. He didn't even know she'd waited. Yet here she is, staring right into Mintzer's face, staring down Mintzer's pinchy, pursed, how-dare-you look, so that even though the last thing in the world Jake wanted was to get chewed out in front of Kira, he feels like whooping for joy.

"I mean, I'm sorry for butting in," she says, with the same cool, I'm-not-sorry-for-anything look she used on people in the subway. "It might seem like Jake was cutting, but the fact is, he was at chorus."

Mintzer stares at her. She gapes at Jake. Her mouth opens, then closes.

Jake has to fight the urge to poke Kira, to say, *Do you see that? She's speechless! She can't say a word!* He's so excited he almost misses what Kira says.

"That's right," she tells Mintzer, "Jake's singing in the chorus. With me."

"I don't know what you're smiling about, Jake," Ms. Mintzer says. "Or you, either, young lady. Jake may want to be in chorus. He may wish he was in chorus. But, until I hear otherwise, he's in my English class. And, until he hears otherwise, he has to deal with me."

"Attitude and Pizzazz"

I get to school extra early the next morning and go to my usual spot by the corner—as far as possible from the main doors, where the girls stand around commenting on everyone who passes, and away from the yard, where the boys call stuff at the girls—across from the grocery store where Jake and Eugene always stand.

I've gotten so used to seeing them there, Eugene fussing with his bagel, Jake reading the headlines on the newspaper rack, that when I finally met them the other day I'd almost stopped feeling like, *Oh, no. Please. Not someone from the subway!* It was more like, *Oh, yeah, there they are again, in their own little private world. I wouldn't mind if they noticed me.*

So, now where is he? It's just Eugene, doing that strange twirly thing with his sleeves, looking like he hates me.

I rub Grandma's horseshoe necklace three times for luck and go up to him. "Where's Jake today?"

Eugene hardly looks at me. "The office. With his parents."

"So, he's really in trouble?"

"Uh, yeah," he says. "Again."

"Again?"

He doesn't say, "And it's your fault," but there's no mistaking it.

We both peer up the block, hoping to spot him.

"I did the best I could, Eugene," I say. "I tried to cover for him."

He looks confused.

I ask, "You didn't hear what happened?"

"I know he cut English again for like the eleventh time. So he could drag me to chorus. And I know he's grounded."

"But he didn't tell you anything?"

He twists his sleeves up again. "They wouldn't let me talk to him. They won't even let him e-mail. All his mom said was they had this meeting and don't wait for him."

"That doesn't sound good." I tell him about the run-in with Jake's teacher.

He curses. "I told him she'd catch him! I told him it was stupid!"

I think about my friend Megan's brother, Tim, and his friends, who played hooky all the time. Tim hid out in his basement and drank beer. That's not Jake. Cutting doesn't seem like Jake, either. "Why'd he do it?"

Eugene's eyebrow goes up. "Would you believe to see you sing?"

"What?" I'm getting that horrible swarmy beetle feeling. "No! You're lying, Eugene! I'm not in the subway anymore. I haven't been there for weeks!" I wonder what else Jake saw besides me singing: that woman offering me her leftover lunch? That man from St. Somebody's asking Dad if we needed a place to stay?

Jake had to have liked me, though, if he kept coming to see me. He had to have really liked me.

"So, what's gonna happen?" I ask Eugene. "Will they suspend him?"

Eugene peers up the block again. "I don't know."

"And I guess the duck didn't help. With his folks and all."

He nods. "The duck that broke the camel's back. Who's about to be turned into Peking Dirk."

Now I'm the confused one.

"Famous Chinese dish?" he says. "The most famous duck dish in the world? Peking Duck? It was a joke, Kira."

Just from the way he says my name, I can tell he wishes they'd never met me.

"Listen," I say. "When you see him later, would you say I'm sorry?"

His eyes soften, but not a lot. He twirls his sleeves loose. "You tell him."

Instead of going straight home that afternoon I find a spot across the street from the Science Center door and wait for Jake. I'm standing there, thinking about something Grandma said last night: "I can't tell if it's them girls down there who are standoffish, or if it's you, Kira," trying not to freeze in Dad's denim jacket, wishing I had something to wear besides that and the puffy periwinkle, when I see the two kids staring at me.

At first I tell myself I'm being paranoid. Only one person at school has recognized me so far— a cafeteria lady who gives me this sort of "Oh, you poor dear" smile when she hands me my lunch—but she's never said anything, so it's possible she just feels sorry I have to eat her nasty food.

I'm not paranoid now, though. The second I hear the girl's voice, I know it's that big-mouth from the subway. She's changed her hair from punk pink to, like, fuzzy rainbow cotton candy.

"Hey, Tyler! Look!" she tells her friend. "Isn't that Amazing Cleo? From the subway platform?"

Her friend looks me over then sticks his lip out and shakes his head. "Uh-uh. That girl was, like, short and skanky."

Say "This girl is short and skanky." I dare you! I tell the bigmouthed girl in my head. If I were back home I *would* tell her. I force myself to meet her stare as they walk up to me.

"You're that subway girl, right?" she says.

No. Yes! No. Buzz off! I'm usually good at coming up with things to say. I make myself as tall as I can. "No," I say. "I'm not. And my name is Kira."

"Told you." Tyler smirks at her.

She makes a shruggy face. "Whatever. See you in the subway."

My pulse has just started coming back to normal when, from across the street, Dad waves to me. He's got Charlie on his shoulders. Chris is holding his hand. They've got one of those red plastic flying-saucer sleds with them.

Still no sign of Jake. Which I'm now glad of.

"Dad!" I say once they're next to me. "What are you doing here?"

"Meeting you at school," he says.

"Why?" They haven't picked me up since my first day.

"I thought we'd take the boys over to the park for a little fun before I leave for work," he says. "Then I promised them you'd go for ice cream."

"Dad." I check for Jake again. "This isn't a good time." I check to make sure Tyler and that girl aren't somewhere around. Or anyone else, for that matter. "I'm sort of waiting for somebody."

"No problem." He lifts Charlie down from his shoulders.

"No!" Charlie whines.

"Dad?" I'm getting a bad feeling here. He's smiling, talking about fun, but neither of the boys has said hi to me. Charlie's crying now. Chris looks about to. Charlie's got Blankie and Passy both; he hasn't taken either one outside in weeks. It's way too cold for the park. "Dad? What's going on?"

"You know how I helped shovel the sidewalk the other day?" he says. "And how I dug out the super's car?"

"Yeah."

He's stopped smiling. I wonder if he lost his job. I take Charlie's hand.

"The super's offered me some work," he says.

"Instead of driving the cab? Really?" I couldn't

care less if he's lost that job if he's got one in our building. *Yeah. Not being alone every night with the boys? Not lying there every night wondering if he's okay, waiting to hear his key turn in the lock? Dad not tired or asleep all the time?* "Dad, that's great, right?"

He makes a Grandma-like snort. "Not great enough. We're only talking maybe an hour or so weekdays, and a couple hours on the weekends. I still have to drive."

I try not to let him see I'm disappointed. "That's okay. What'll you be doing?"

"Maintenance stuff. Pulling garbage. Whatever. He'll pay me cash."

There's another shoe waiting to drop. I can feel it.

"Chris," he says. "Take Charlie and go sit over on that stoop a minute, okay?"

"No." Chris presses closer to him. "I don't want to."

"Okay, buddy. That's cool." He turns back to me. "You know your stepmom?"

"Yeah . . ." No one's called Tammy my stepmom since she and Dad moved down to the city and didn't take me.

"I gave her the fifty bucks I made."

"What?" I knew he'd talked to her a few times and that it didn't go well. I didn't think he'd seen her. "When?"

"Just now." He lowers his voice. "She paid us a visit."

"Why? What for? Is she coming back to you?" I don't know if that'd be good or not. I used to think Tammy was so cool. I'd be, like, "When's Tammy coming? When's Tammy coming?" Then, after she and Dad left, I'd be wanting to look like her, dress like her, sing like her. I didn't care what Grandma and Aunt Phyllis said about her. And when I first got here, and was so pissed at Dad, I could sort of see why she left him. Now I kind of hate her. "Does she want to? Are you guys getting back together?"

His mouth tightens. "She says I owe her money."

"We don't have any money."

"I told her. But she said things aren't going that good with her and—"

"Yeah, well, join the club! I can't believe she had the nerve to tell you that! So then what happened?"

I definitely hate her.

I hate this shrug of his, too.

"I gave her the fifty bucks."

"And then what?"

"He told her we had to pick you up at school," Chris says in a small voice. "He said we were going to the park."

"And she just left? She didn't want to come with you?" I say before I see Dad's eyes go from the boys to me, warning me off.

He picks Charlie up again and, with his other arm, pulls Chris to him. "She wanted to come," he says so gently I know it's baloney. "But she couldn't. She had to go. But she'll be back to see you. She promised you that, right, buddy?"

Chris doesn't answer.

Dad tips Chris's chin up. "She'll be back, Chris. She's coming next week. I told her I'm working steady now," he tells me. "I said if she came by I'd pay her a little something every—"

"What? After she ran off and left you for—"

"Rodney," he finishes for me.

"Rodney? His name is Rodney?" I don't know why that pisses me off so much. "She walked out on her kids"—I shouldn't be saying this with them here listening—"for some loser bass player named Rodney—"

"Drummer, actually."

"While you drive a cab twelve hours a night to keep us going? And now you'll be working two jobs?" My ears are totally floating. "I mean here we are, we're finally starting to get things . . . we're trying so hard . . ."

"I know, Ki." He sighs and pulls Chris closer. "Hey, worst case? I can always go back to singing in the subway. A bad song is better than no song, right?"

I glare at him. "What does that mean?"

He shrugs again. "You think I know? Come on, guys. Let's go to the park now and have some fun. Let's all go to the park."

We've just started walking when I see Jake and Eugene a half block ahead of us, trudging along like their backpacks are loaded down with rocks. Things must not be good.

Well, join the club, I think again. I wouldn't mind if my biggest problem was being grounded and finding a home for a duck.

Then I think, *Home for a duck?*

The timing sucks, but as Grandma would say, when you can't do something about the big stuff, find something you *can* do. I feel through my jacket for her horseshoe necklace and touch it three times for luck. "Stay right here, okay?" I tell Dad. "Guys, I'll just be a minute. I'll be right back. I promise. I have to talk to somebody."

"Do you still have the duck?" I say when I catch up with Jake and Eugene.

Jake jumps.

"Oh. Sorry. I just had this idea." I check to make

sure Dad hasn't followed me. I'm going to need to prepare Dad for this. And for them. "You all right?"

Jake nods.

"So, what happened at your meeting? Did it come out okay? Are you in a lot of trouble?"

He doesn't answer.

"But you can be in chorus, right?"

"That's the good news," Eugene tells me. "For him, anyway."

"And I'm th-th-th- . . . rough with Mintzer," Jake adds. "I'm out of her class!" He smiles at me.

"Well, I'm glad there's some good news," I tell him. "I'm not sure I can take any more bad news today!" I check to see how Dad's doing. He's sat down on a stoop. He's got both boys on his lap. I suddenly feel ashamed of not wanting to be seen with him. "Listen," I say. "You guys want to come to the park with us now?"

"Can't," Eugene says, looking at Jake.

Whew! "Oh. Right. You're grounded. Sorry. Remember how I told you the people down the road have ducks?"

"What road?" Eugene asks as Jake nods.

"My road back home. They're big duck people," I tell Jake. "They might want Dirk. I talk to my grandmother every night. I'll ask her." I dig around in my backpack for a pencil and paper to write down our number. "She calls every night on her lunch break. So if you call at, like, seven or eight . . ."

"Uh . . ." Jake looks down at his shoes.

"Oh, right," I say again. "No calls. What about if I call you? I can tell them it's duck business."

He looks even more embarrassed.

"Fine," I say. "No problem. Just tell your mom you've found a place for him. If you work it out with her, I'll deal with my dad." *What am I doing?* I think as I write down my address and hand it to him. *This is even stupider than Jake cutting English.* "Yeah. Tomorrow's Saturday. Bring Dirk over tomorrow."

Jake looks at me. "You may have just saved a life."

"Oh, sure! Why not?" Dad says when I get back to them. "Sure! Bring him on. With all the troubles we've got, what's a duck more or less? Hell, why wait for tomorrow? Tell him to bring it right now. I like duck. We'll have it for Sunday dinner."

"Thank you, Dad! Thank you so much!" I don't care that he's being sarcastic. Or that I have no idea what Grandma will say when I ask her to drive down to get Dirk. Jake looked so relieved and grateful. "It'll just be till we can figure out how to get him to Claryville."

He lifts the boys off his lap. "Guess we're not going to the park then. We better find a box before I have to leave for work." He checks his watch. "Yeah. Sorry, guys. It's kinda cold for sledding anyway."

"I'll take them sledding tomorrow." I'm already picturing all of us going: *me, Jake, the boys. And Dad?* "Dad," I say as he hoists Charlie onto his shoulders again and we start walking. "You are gonna be nice to him, right? You won't say anything about the sub-way?" I'm thinking about how if Grandma comes down when Jake's there, or even Jake and Eugene, she'll see that I am making friends. Even if they're not girls. Even if they're totally not what she's used to.

"Uh . . . speaking of Grandma," Dad says. "I'd feel a little better if we leave your grandma out of this for now. Go ahead and tell her about the duck, if you want, but I'd just as soon she didn't come rushing down here with this whole Tammy thing brewing."

"Brewing?" I stop thinking about tomorrow for a second. "What's brewing?"

"I don't mean brewing," he says. "There's noth-ing brewing. It's just that she didn't think that highly of Tammy at the best of times. And I'm not sure I ever mentioned about me owing her money."

"So then what happens to Dirk?"

"Chris." He pulls Chris's hat up so he can see his eyes, and tugs Charlie's foot. "Chazman. How'd you guys like a pet?"

CHAPTER 16

"I think he may have thrown up in his cage," Eugene announces as soon as they arrive the next morning. He's carrying a giant bag of duck chow.

Jake's carrying the cage. He looks around the living room, which, even though I got up early and did my best to fix it up, is, except for Dad's instrument corner, its usual shabby self.

"Morning," I say.

Jake nods. He seems as nervous as I am.

"He didn't like the cab at all," Eugene tells Dad, who's just come back from pulling garbage. "He was, like, quacking nonstop, and then the quacking stopped, and there was this disgusting smell, I mean, way worse than his usual smell. . . ."

"Just don't let it out in here, okay?" Dad tells Jake, who's put the cage down and started looking at the instruments. "I got a lot of valuable equipment in this room."

"Yeah. Whoa, you do have a lot of instruments,"

Eugene says. "And here I thought you were just a subway singer. You're, like, a real musician."

Jake gives him a dirty look.

Dad looks at me.

"Oops," Eugene says. "Sorry. I have a mouth problem sometimes." He looks at Jake again. "Uh-oh. That came out wrong too." He turns to Charlie, who's been hiding behind Dad's leg. "Hey, there. When is a duck not a duck?"

Charlie just stares at him.

"When he's a Dirky?" Eugene says. "Get it? Dirky? Turkey?"

Dad rolls his eyes at me, but he doesn't say anything.

Chris, however, says, "I get it!"

"Okay, then," Eugene says to him. "What kind of cereal do ducks like?"

"Quackios!" Chris says.

Eugene nods. "I'd have said, Snap, Quackle, and Pop. I like yours better!"

"Guys," Dad says. "Let's get this duck out to the backyard. Chris, tell them about the surprise."

"It's a pool!" Chris tells Eugene.

Charlie peeks out from behind Dad's leg again. "For Dirk!"

"It's not a real backyard," I tell Jake as we walk

down the hall. I can't stop thinking about how big and beautiful his apartment was, with the fireplace and the doorman and the lobby with rugs and real flowers. "And the pool's just one of those plastic kiddy things," I add as Dad opens the back door onto the area between the front section of the basement, where our apartment is, and the back section. "But it's all ready. We dumped the snow out and filled it with water."

We also put the old ironing board and stuff out on the street and shoveled all the snow into the corners. And the day is warming up fast. The sun's so bright that, just in the time since we came out, the snow's melted off the picnic table and you can see pavement.

"So, Jake, you gonna do the honors?" Dad says, nodding toward the pool.

Jake holds the cage over it and opens the door.

Splash! Dirk's in the water. The boys jump back squealing as he rears up and flaps his wings.

"Oh, wow!" Eugene says as the duck settles in and starts swimming in circles. "That is one happy little ducky!"

Jake looks at me. "A l-l-l-lucky ducky."

It's the first thing he's said since he got here.

It's also the first time since yesterday I've seen Chris or Charlie smile.

"He's not a ducky," Chris tells Eugene. "He's a dirky!"

Eugene laughs. Dad smiles. I don't see any throw-up in the cage. I start to relax a little.

"Now," Dad says, "if we can knock together some sort of duck house for him . . ."

"We're building Dirk a house?" It's the first I've heard of this. "What about that box we found for him?"

"That was before I saw all the wood and stuff in Ivan's shop just now," he says. "You guys feel like helping?"

Jake gives Eugene a quick glance. "Sure."

"Excellent!" Dad unlocks the steel door that leads to the basement. "I'll go see what I can scrounge up. It's warm enough to work outside, right?"

"Sure," Jake says again.

"Uh, Jake?" Eugene taps his watch.

Jake frowns at him. "We're fine," he tells Dad.

"Great!" Dad says. "Ki, go grab the boys' boots and jackets so they don't catch cold out here. I'll be right back."

The four boys are crouched around the pool

when I return. Chris and Charlie are tossing in pieces of duck chow, giggling as Dirk snaps them up.

"Hey, Chris," Eugene says as I squat down next to him and stuff Chris's arms into his parka. "Did you know you could teach ducks to talk?"

"Yes!" Chris says in a sassy voice. He leans on my shoulder and lifts his foot so I can take off his sneaker and put on his boot.

"Okay, then, wise guy," Eugene says. "What does the duck say when you teach him to talk?"

Chris lifts his other leg for me. "Quack!" he tells Eugene.

"No!" Eugene says as I move on to Charlie. "Polly want a quacker. What do ducks like for snack?"

Charlie squirms out of my grasp. "Quackios!"

"Wrong!" Eugene sings back at him. "Cheese and quackers!"

"Yuck, yuck," I say, grabbing Charlie again to do up his zipper. "You're quacking me up, Eugene." But I can't help smiling at him, seeing how nice he is with the boys. "I'd have never figured Eugene for someone who likes kids," I tell Jake as he and I stand up and walk over to the picnic table. "And Dirk looks like he's died and gone to heaven."

Jake nods. "It's so cool you're doing this."

"It's sort of a miracle it's working out." *Knock wood,* I can hear Grandma adding. Or maybe it was rubbing her good luck charm all those times. "How're things working out for you?"

He doesn't answer.

"I'm sorry if I got you in more trouble with your teacher. I didn't mean to."

He picks at some peeling paint on the table. "It wasn't you. I'm f-f-f-fine."

"That's good. And Eugene said yesterday they *are* letting you guys be in chorus."

"Uh . . . Everyone who thinks he's fine take one step forward," Eugene calls over to us. "Not so fast, Kandell—"

"Shut up, Eugene!" Jake calls back. "D-D-D-Don't listen to him!" he tells me. "I am f-f-f-fine. And I am in chorus."

"So then . . ." I take a deep breath. "You'll be going on Monday?"

He nods.

"Because you know . . ." I've been gearing up for this for two days. I'm surprised how nervous I am. "When I said that to your teacher the other day . . . about me being in chorus? I—"

"The Mighty Mintzmobile?" Eugene cuts in.

"Yo, Chris. Here's one! What does Jake say when he sees the Mintzmobile rolling down the hall?"

"Shut up, Eugene!" Jake's face is bright red. I'd thought they were just joking around before, but he looks hopping mad.

Eugene ignores him. "When Jake sees the Mintzmobile rolling down the hall, he yells"—Eugene wraps his arms over his head—"'Duck it!'"

"Duck it!" Chris shouts.

"Duck it in the bucket!" Charlie yells.

Jake stomps over to the pool. "What about sh-sh-sh-shut up d-d-d-don't you g-g-g-get, Eugene? Sh-sh-sh-shut up means shut up! Kira's trying to—"

"What're you yelling at me for?" Eugene's voice sounds hurt. "What'd I say? I didn't say anything. Kira, did I say anything?"

The basement door opens. "You guys having a problem?" Dad says, propping it open with his foot. He's carrying a stack of boards. He has a huge grin on his face.

"No." Jake glares at Eugene. "No problem."

"Excellent. Give me a hand, then, would you?" Dad says. "You wouldn't believe how much wood Ivan has back there!"

Jake and Eugene silently help him set the

boards down on the picnic table. Then they all head back inside for more.

"Why'd Jake yell at him?" Chris asks me as I get Charlie's jacket zipped.

"I guess he thinks Eugene's not funny," I tell him.

"Eugene's funny!" Charlie says. "I like Eugene!"

"Why doesn't Jake like him?" Chris says.

"He does like him," I say. "They're best friends. It's just . . . I don't know."

And I sort of don't want to.

"I'm figuring we'll make it just like a doghouse, right?" Dad says when they get back. He's got more lumber. Eugene's lugging a large red metal toolbox. Jake's carrying what looks to be a screw gun. "If we run an extension cord out a basement window and hook up a lightbulb for him, we can keep him warm enough so he can pretty much live outside. So, Gene," he says. "How're you with a hammer and saw? Because I know Kira's pretty good. Right, Ki? Kira grew up on a farm."

"Uh . . ." Eugene looks embarrassed. "Unless you count Kim's Green Farm . . ."

Dad turns to Jake. "You done any woodworking?"

He's clearly waiting for Jake to say no, too, but Jake nods. "Yeah!" he says. "My dad and I—"

"Good deal!" Dad interrupts. "So then you and Ki can work together. Gene, since you're doing so great with the duck and the boys, why don't you be in charge of them. Feel free to take the boys inside anytime."

"Fine," Eugene says stiffly. He doesn't look at Jake. "I can do that."

No. I definitely don't want to know. Things are going so amazingly well this morning. The boys are having the best time they've had since I don't know when. Dad too. I just want to enjoy being out here with all of us and have a nice, calm, peaceful, normal time.

CHAPTER 17

The sun is high enough now that we can work without my hands and feet freezing. Dad gives us our instructions. We lay everything out and start measuring. He takes the frame and the roof. Jake and I work on the sides. At first I look up every minute or so to make sure Eugene and the boys are okay. Then I just work. I forgot how much fun it is to build things. I haven't done anything like this since my grandpa and I built bluebird houses right before he died. And I'm amazed how good Jake is with tools.

Except to say *Could you hand me the whatever?* or *How's this look to you?* we work quietly. Eugene and the boys come over a few times to check it out and then they go inside. By noon, we've got the parts ready. Dad assembles it with the screw gun. Amazingly, it goes together perfectly. "Look at that!" I say as Dad lugs it to a corner of the yard and we walk around inspecting it from all sides. "It's not wonky. It's square! It's beautiful! We did it!"

"Of course we did it!" Dad brushes sawdust off my front and claps Jake on the back. "Who's cooler than us!"

Jake beams back at him.

Dad opens the apartment door. "Guys! Come outside! Are we cool, or what?" he asks Jake again as Chris and Charlie come running. "Yo, Dirk! Is this the most fantastic duck house you have ever seen?"

Dirk is way too happy in his pool to care, but Chris and Charlie immediately crawl inside. Dad has to promise to make everyone an eyeball surprise to coax them out again.

"We should go now," Eugene says once we're finally back in the apartment. It's almost the first thing he's said since Jake went off on him.

"You're not gonna stay for my famous eyeball surprise?" Dad looks disappointed. "I saw you checking out my instruments before. You don't want to see 'em?"

Jake looks at Eugene. "Sure," he says.

Eugene looks back at him.

"Oh, and I came up with a new song last night," Dad tells Jake. "Kind of a ballad. I haven't dared try it on Ki yet. Ki's my toughest critic."

Jake looks at Eugene again. "You could . . . try it on us," he says.

Before I can say anything, Dad's over at the kitchen table with his guitar, tuning, with Chris and Charlie next to him and Jake behind him. Eugene stays by the couch.

"Why am I still writing all these love songs," Dad sings,

> *"When I got no one to sing my love songs to?*
> *I lie in my bed, these songs messing with*
>   *my head,*
> *It's a shame, babe, I'm still writing them*
>   *for you."*

"Dad?" It's a shame all right. And he really said he wrote this yesterday?

> *"Every time I pick my pen up, or reach for*
>   *my guitar . . ."*

And why would he bring up Tammy now, when we're all finally having such a good time? "Dad?" This time I tap his shoulder.

Dad winks at Jake. "See what I mean, man?"

"I'm not tough!" I tell him. "I like the song, Dad. I like the chords and the melody—"

"But the lyrics suck."

"They don't suck. It's just that . . ."—I search for a nonmean way to say it—"they make you sound so . . ."

"Pitiful?" He starts again:

> *Why am I still writing all these love songs*
> *When they make me sound like one*
>   *pathetic dude?*

"Gene," he says. "Help me out here, man. Food? Rude? Mood?"

"Huh?" Eugene says. "Sorry. I wasn't listening."

"Why am I still writing all these love songs," Jake sings so softly I can hardly hear him. "When my songs make me sound like such a jerk? . . ." He eyes Dad nervously.

"Why you stopping?" Dad says. "You're not hurting my feelings. Go on. Let's hear this!"

"Why am I still writing all these love songs . . ." Jake sings it louder this time.

No wonder he wants to be in chorus! He's got a really good voice!

"When the person I'm writing about is such a jerk?"

Uh-oh. I look over at the boys. They don't seem to know Jake is singing about their mom.

"There you go!" Dad says, clapping. "I like that!"

"There you go!" Charlie cries.

And when he finishes up with: "But lyrics never suck when you sing them to a duck. Especially when the ducky's name is Dirk!" I clap too.

Jake makes a stupid face, but his eyes are shining.

And then the doorbell rings. Jake's face goes white.

Eugene curses. The boys race for the door. Dad goes to open it.

"Sorry to barge in like this," the woman in the entryway tells him. She's really pretty. She's got on jeans and a beautiful suede jacket. She looks a lot like Jake. "I'm Lynn Kandell," she says. "Is Jake still here, by any chance?"

"Sure, come on in!" Dad says. "We just finished building a duck house. I was about to fix everyone some eggs. Not duck eggs, I'm sorry to say, but you're welcome. Come in," he says again, because she hasn't. "Excuse the mess. It's—"

"Maybe another time," she says. "It was extremely nice of you to agree to take the duck, and go to all this trouble, but I'm afraid Jake has somewhere he needs to be. He was supposed to be home an hour ago. Jake! Let's go!" Her voice isn't nearly as polite now. She steps into the living room. Oh, man, does she look mad. "I thought we had a deal," she tells him. "I thought we agreed that you would drop off the duck and come right home to get ready for your appointment. You know Dr. Stone didn't have to agree to see us on a Saturday. . . ."

Oh. No wonder Eugene was bugging him.

Jake doesn't say anything. He doesn't look at her.

"Get your jacket, Jake," she says. "If we leave right now we might still be able to make it."

He doesn't move.

Eugene looks as petrified as he does. "Should I come with you?" he whispers.

"What exactly do you think this is accomplishing, Jake?" she says as Eugene picks up his own jacket. "All this running?"

I can see Jake swallow. I can almost feel his jaws tighten.

"I'm-m-m-m- . . ."

Most of the time when he stutters my mind sort of skips over it. I know he's doing it, but I just kind of hang out and wait for it to pass.

"M-m-m- . . ."

It's not passing. It's like his jaws are glued shut. Or like he's trying to start a car and it won't start.

"Ki!" Charlie tugs on my arm. "What's he doing? What's wrong with him?"

"Nothing," I tell him in my Grandma voice. "He's fine."

He was, a minute ago. A minute ago he sang perfectly. He sounded great. And sometimes he talks perfectly, better than I do. Smarter. Funnier.

He keeps jerking his head, like it'll shake his jaws open, or shake the words out. His eyes keep darting to the ceiling, as if he's praying.

"Jake, man," Dad says. "It's okay. Take it easy. It ain't worth it, man. Relax. We had a great time today, right? So don't worry about it. You can come back anytime." He turns to Jake's mom. "You shoulda heard him sing before. I mean, this kid can—"

"You need to breathe, honey," his mom says. She doesn't look mad anymore. She looks like she's trying not to cry. "You're not breathing. See, Jake. This is why we're going for this consultation now. Exactly for this reason. So you don't have to keep going through this all the time."

We should not be watching this. I feel like all of us should leave. But it seems worse to walk away from him. And he's so determined. He just won't give up.

I want to go over and take his hand. But if it were me up there in front of everyone, I'd probably slap my hand down. So I take Charlie's hand instead, and force myself not to look away.

Just when I think it can't go on, that he's going to turn blue and fall on the floor, his breath explodes out of him. He looks at the ceiling again. Then, as my hand goes to my neck and I touch Grandma's horseshoe, he says, so softly that I can hardly hear it, "I . . . wasn't . . . r-r-r-running."

He walks over and picks up his jacket, and with a look in his eyes I know really well—it's the same I-will-get-through-this—And-not-only-that—I'll-be-cool look I've been working on for years—he turns to me. "S-S-S-See you at c-c-c-chorus," he says.

CHAPTER 18

I'm so nervous Monday morning I squeeze hand cream on my toothbrush instead of Colgate. I haven't opened my mouth to sing since Pajama Pants.

Or maybe it's not totally about chorus. Or totally nervousness. I might also be excited. All I know is when Dirk starts quacking at ten minutes to five Monday morning, I'm wide awake. Then, because I want to do something about something, and I can't think of anything besides calling Grandma— which is a bad idea even if she's up, since last night when she asked, as always, if everything was under control, I said it was—I cut my hair.

I don't set out to make it an inch long. I trim off the split ends. Then I even both sides. Then I try bangs and I hate the bangs, so I cut them off. And that looks totally stupid till I cut the rest shorter. And so on, till I look in the mirror and go, *Whoa. This is definitely not Subway Girl. This is not Amazing Cleo.* Once I've survived Dad's lawnmower

jokes, I stop on the way to school and, with some of
the emergency money Grandma gave me, buy a jar
of wax to spike it up. I also spot a bargain bin full of
little makeup samples, so instead of going to meet
Jake and Eugene across from school, I head for the
girls' room. And then I look really different. Which
actually does make things feel a little more under
control.

Even so, by the time sixth period comes, my heart
is thumping as hard as the hip-hop music playing
in the auditorium. Some girls are up on stage dancing. Two boys are wrestling over the microphone.
I'm glad to see I don't recognize any of them. "Be
advised, children!" the one who gets the mike says
in a crazy voice. "I'm in a ferocious mood today. Do
not try my patience." A few kids laugh, but most are
too busy roaming around, eating their lunches, and
chatting to care. Or notice me, I'm glad to see. "Now
I'm going to teach you a hundred and three new
songs today, people!" the boy says.

  Whew! There's Jake, in the third row, with
Eugene. He spots me and waves.

  "Hey," he says, shoving the remains of his sandwich in his backpack when I slide in next to him.

  "Hey," I say. I can't tell what he thinks of my

new hair. Or the lipstick and eyeliner. A couple of girls so far have said it was cool. But I also spotted that cotton-candy haired girl gawking at me in the hall. "How's it going, Eugene?"

"Okay." He looks at Jake. "So far, anyway."

"How's Dirk?" Jake says. "Does he like his house?"

"Yeah." I'm about to add: How was it when you left Saturday? Is everything okay? But something in his eyes stops me. "His pool froze last night. We had to bring him inside to the hall." I wonder what happened with his mom after they left.

Eugene leans across him. "I like your hair."

Jake nods. "M-M-M-Me, too. You l-l-l-look so . . ."

"Punk?" I say as he hunts for a word. "Bald? Like I got run over by a lawnmower?"

"No. Uh-uh," he says. "Different. For a s-s-s-second I wasn't sure it was you."

I'm about to say "Good!" when the music clicks off. The kids jump from the stage and race to find seats. Ms. Hill walks in through the stage door.

She's not as old as Grandma, but she's not young. Her hair, cut really close and worn natural, is dotted with gray. She's got on large, dangling, silver disk earrings and billowy black pants, and a floaty cowl-neck top in a lime green that would make me look like a corpse, but looks great against her deep brown skin. She's not tall or thin or beautiful; she's not even wearing makeup; but there's something about her. Sort of like someone's just turned on all the lights.

She also looks familiar. I've seen her somewhere.

"Who was just on my mike?" she says as the beetles start swarming through my veins.

Maybe in the halls at school? Or I could be imagining it. Why don't I think so?

"Whoever it was," she says, "please stand."

Even that actressy voice sounds familiar to me.

"Now leave," she tells the boy. "I've got no time for nonsense, people," she says as he scuttles for the door. "You know I have a lot of anger inside me. You get me started, we don't know what I'll do. Isn't that right?" She looks down the rows of kids. Her eyes stop on . . . *No. Please. Don't do this to me in front of everyone!* "What's your name again, baby?"

Eugene shoots us a quick *uh-oh* look. "Eugene Kim."

"Of course!" She smiles at him. "How could I have forgotten? How *are* you today, Eugene? You must have liked us the other day. You liked us so much you came back and brought your friend.

That's good. It's very good." She smiles at him again, then at Jake, and then, for an endless second, at me. Then she says, "Step up and get your music, people. Do it fast and do it quietly. We have a lot of ground to cover and no accompanist today."

"And there'll be no more wise quacks out of you, young man," Eugene whispers as we follow the other kids to the box of music on the piano. Why he insists on filling his pockets full of Nik Naks, which clink and rattle with every step . . .

We're hardly back in our seats when she starts the exercises. "Lip trills!" she says, doing this loud *Brrr!* thing into the microphone. "Yes, I know it makes your lips itch. And don't look at your neighbors or you're going to laugh! Sips!" she calls next. "Sip in some air. Little sips. Hold it. And now let it out slowly, like a leaky tire. Slowly! *Ssss* . . ." I look around and try to do what everyone else is doing. "Squeals, now, starting high, as high as you can go . . ."

I hated the singing exercises Ms. Briggs made us do. *Stand up straight, boys and girls!* Not that there were many boys in that chorus. *Arms by your sides! Repeat after me: "Diction-is-done-with-the-tip-of-the-tongue-and-your-teeth."* Ms. Hill's exercises are so crazy they're fun. I also hated the music we sang:

"Alas my luh-huve you dooo me wrong . . ."
I hated the way we sang a song, and sang it, and
sang it, and sang it—la la, blah blah—till I was ready
to fall off the stage. I hated the way Ms. Briggs
looked at me, like, *Love the voice! Now if we could
just do something about you.* I hated the way the
Goody Two-shoes girls in chorus always thought
I was showing off. This is such a big chorus I
don't even have to try not to stick out.

"'Alegría!'" Ms. Hill calls. "If you remember it
from last year, sing along. Or read it off your part,
if you think you can. If you're not sure, make like a
submarine. Put your little periscope up every once
in a while, and when you need to, dive back under."

"Think I'll dive under and stay under," Eugene
says as she steps to the piano and gives us
our pitches. She hasn't seated us in sections. She
doesn't seem to care. She picks up the microphone
and starts to sing. "Alegrí, alegrí, alegría . . ."

I knew she'd have a good voice. You just have to
see her to know that. But there's good, and then
there's so gorgeous it blows you away.

Like me, I think before I can help myself.

As we start singing Jake smiles at me again. It's
amazing how different he looks when he sings. His
forehead unscrunches. His face smoothes out. His

eyes shine. Not to mention that he's reading the notes off his part, singing along perfectly. Unlike me, who sings pretty much by ear. "You've sung this before, right?" I whisper to him.

"Uh-uh." He shakes his head.

"Let's keep this moving!" Ms. Hill says. "Everyone turn to 'Into the Light.' I'll sing it through for you."

I can't get over how beautiful her voice is.

But I'm just starting to get the melody in my head when she's on to something else.

She stands us up. She sits us down. We do another exercise. We do another song. We hurry up to the stage and form a semicircle. We hustle to our chairs. She tells us we're slumping, slouching, not concentrating, out of tune, out to lunch, unacceptable, barely acceptable. Which really surprises me, because this chorus is a hundred times better than the one at home. There are some good singers in this chorus. *As good as me, though?* I can't help thinking. And in fact, the one time she actually calls out, "Yes! Now, you're getting it," I could swear she's looking at me.

So, when the period is over and she walks up to us with her eyes sparkling, every compliment I've ever gotten floods into my head: *Kira's a natural.*

Kira's a big talent. She's got a fantastic ear. She's got perfect pitch. That voice is a gift from God! Kira, you sing like an angel!

"Eugene Kim," Ms. Hill says, "I like you."

Eugene looks even more shocked than I am. "You do?"

She nods. "I like your verve, Eugene. Of course, you've got some other issues we'll need to work on. And you . . ." She turns to Jake. "Jake, right?" He nods. "You love to sing, Jake, don't you? I can tell. You're so concentrated. And you're a good sight-reader!"

My heart pounds as she looks at me.

"Welcome!" she says. "I'm so glad to have you here. Welcome! I love your hair."

What? I think as the beetles start up again. *She didn't ask my name. Is that because she thinks it's Cleo? From the subway? Or does my singing suck?*

I know that can't be true.

"Oh, Jake, darling!" Eugene gushes as soon as we walk out. "You are just so vervacious!" He slaps his forehead. "Oh, no, right. That's *me*! *You're* the concentrated one. Jake, baby, I *love* your concentr—"

"So, what'd you think?" Jake asks me. His face is still glowing from her compliment. "It was good, right? Did you like it? Did you s-s-s-see the way Ms.

177

Hill was looking at you? When you were singing?"

"Kira's dumbstruck," Eugene says when I don't answer. "She can't believe my vervacity."

Jake looks at him. "Not d-d-d-dumbstruck, dummy! Songstruck! She can't wait till Th-Th-Th-Thursday. So she can go again."

She didn't have to have seen me in the subway. She could have noticed me in the halls. Maybe there's some singer radar thing where singers can spot other singers. That would be cool, actually. That would be very cool. Or it's possible she really does love my hair. I just wish I knew.

CHAPTER 19

But Ms. Hill doesn't say a word to me the next time, or the next few times. After a few weeks I stop waiting for the other shoe to drop. Girls are beginning to smile at me when I arrive. I'm getting used to her: "Ex*cuse* me?" It cracks me up how she always sweeps in with this big warning that she's in a vicious mood, and then isn't. I love all her colors, and the way everything she wears swirls or flaps or floats; how her earrings are at least ten times bigger than any teacher's I've ever seen; how she calls people "darling" and "baby" and "lady," except for Eugene, who she calls Mr. Nik Nak or, one time, Mr. Mouth. I love that she doesn't make us sit by sections, so that even when I'm singing the soprano part and Jake and Eugene are singing alto, we can sit together.

I also like that we meet during lunch. No more having to walk into the lunchroom by myself, worrying who I'll eat with. Chorus days I don't set foot in there. The other three days I eat with Jake and Eugene, even if Eugene sometimes does try to make me eat mysterious veggie items from his folks' store. Even if a few times I have to eat with him alone because Jake isn't there. Even if that cotton candy-haired girl—who I really am going to tell off one of these days—looks at me like, Eeew, is Eugene your boyfriend?

"He's occupied," he tells me the first time I ask where Jake is. He has a strange look on his face, as if he's either trying to look cool, or is glad Jake isn't here. Could Eugene be getting a crush on me? Is that girl on to something? That's a scary thought.

"Occupied?" I occupy myself with my cheese sandwich. "With what?"

"Stuff."

"What stuff?"

He shrugs. "You know. Stuff he hates. Hateful school stuff. How's Dirk? Does he ask about me?"

"Uh-huh," I say. "He says, 'Where's the quackpot?'"

But the next time I ask where Jake is, Eugene tells me: "Jake's at speech therapy. It was part of that deal they made. You know, the whole Mintzer thing. His mom's making him go to the school speech lady Mondays and Wednesdays. Just don't tell him I told you."

"Why not?"

He makes a face. "It's supposed to be a secret."

"Why?"

He makes another face. "I don't know. You could ask him, but I don't recommend it."

But I'm only stuck alone with Eugene twice. Then Jake's back at lunch with us. He doesn't say a word about speech therapy, though, so I take Eugene's advice and keep my mouth shut.

And if Eugene does have a crush on me, he keeps it to himself.

By the time a few more weeks go by, I can't wait for chorus days. Chris and Charlie can sing all the songs. Dirk probably knows them too. I'm walking around with chorus songs in my head all day long. I'm going on and on about it to Grandma. "Sounds to me," she says, "like this chorus is turning out to be the best thing in your life."

Grandma and I are having our usual daily suppertime phone conversation one evening—"What are you eating?" "More of that casserole. I still haven't figured out how to cook for just me. What'd you fix the boys? Tell me not mac and cheese again, Kira!"— when there's a rap on the back door. Ivan the super. I leave Chris and Charlie at the table and run to get it.

"Your dad's not around, is he?" Ivan sounds pissed.

"Hold on," I tell Grandma. "He's at work," I tell Ivan. "You need me to call him?" Dad and I each have a cell phone now, which is great.

"I just tried him," Ivan says. "I've been trying him. He ran the battery down on my drill again. And I can't find my screw gun. I knocked this morning, but he didn't answer."

"He must have been sleeping," I tell him. "I can leave him a note."

"Do that!" he says. "And while you're at it, remind him he owes me. Maybe if he sees it in writing it'll get through to him."

"Owes you for what?" I ask, forgetting Grandma's still on the line.

"For that lumber he took without asking me," Ivan says. "That was clear pine he used for that goose house of yours. You know how much that cost?" I shake my head. Dad hasn't said a word. "A lot!" he says. "Tell him starting Friday it comes out of his pay. Unless he don't want the job. You can tell him that, too!"

"No. He'll pay you," I promise Ivan. "He'll pay you by Friday." I'm afraid to ask how much.

"What's going on?" Grandma says when he leaves.

I groan. "It's a long story."

She snorts. "With Russell, there's always a long story."

"That's not true," I tell her. "He's been so great lately."

But she's on the phone to him first thing the next morning, which she hasn't done since I started school.

"Relax, Ma," I hear him telling her when I come into the kitchen. "He won't fire me. I'll pay him. It's just . . . I'm a little strapped right now. Tammy's been by a few more times." His voice rises. "No! I know, Ma! I know what I said. But I had to help her out. Ma, do I really need you on my case?"

"Tammy?" I say when he gets off, finally.

"Don't you start with me too, Kira!" he barks. "I got all the women on my back I can handle right now."

I'm still upset when I get to chorus that afternoon. And it seems as if I'm not the only one. Jake and Eugene look terrible.

"Well, what'd you think would happen?" Eugene is telling Jake as I slide in next to him. "I mean, she's called the Mighty Mintzmobile for a reason."

"What are you guys talking about?" I ask as I unwrap my lunch. "What's up?"

Jake glares at Eugene. "Nothing's up."

"Fine," I tell him. "Just don't bark at me, okay? I'm not having too good a day myself."

But then Ms. Hill sails in announcing, as always, how irritable she's feeling, and, as always, I start to get into it.

After warm-ups, she hands out parts for a song I don't know, a piece they worked on in the fall. She sings it through for us. Ms. Bolden plays each part on the piano, so I've got a pretty good idea how it goes. It's like stuff we sang in church choir. And it's in four parts: soprano one, soprano two, and two altos. I'm singing first soprano, the way I always do. Jake's next to me, as usual, singing alto.

I keep up really well for the first few lines, when my part has the melody. But then it goes off and does something complicated, and I'm lost. All I see is a bunch of little black notes. I have no clue how to find my place. And the notes go by so fast. Jake's singing away. Eugene's singing away. But they're singing a different part, which is no help.

So I sing my own notes. I listen to what everyone else is singing and fit my line on top, like when I harmonize with Dad, except I'm doing it with Jake, blending my voice to his and to all the other voices. It works, too. We sound beautiful.

But that's not what makes me so happy, suddenly. It's like I'm not me anymore. Or not just me. I can feel it in Jake, too. His bad mood's completely gone; I don't even have to look at him to know that. I see exactly what Ms. Hill means now when she says, "If you're not sure of your part, make like a submarine." Except I'm not submerged; I'm swimming. I'm floating on the music. I am the music. It feels so beautiful.

For a second, when she raps on her music stand, I think she's going to say that. She's not smiling, though. "Excuse me!" Everyone stops singing. "Excuse me. Someone's not singing the notes!"

She doesn't stare right at me. She doesn't have to.

"I don't care how celestial your voice is," she says. "Or how gorgeous your notes are, if they're the wrong ones. You have to sing your part the way it's written. This is not some little pop song, people. There's no ad-libbing here. This is not improv."

Okay. I get it. You can stop now, I want to tell her. *I got it the first time!*

"It's a Bach chorale, children. Johann Sebastian Bach wrote the voices this way for a reason. If you can't sing your part, don't sing! It's as simple as that."

You're right. It's simple. You don't want me to sing, I won't sing. She probably thinks all I can sing is "I Believe I Can Fly." Why did I even join this stupid chorus?

I don't open my mouth for the rest of the period.

The instant rehearsal's over, I head for the door.

"Where you rushing to, Kira?" she calls to me. She puts an arm around me and steers me to a corner. I'm stiff as a board. "Jake, Eugene"—she waves them over—"come talk to me a minute."

Right. So they can watch me be even more humiliated.

She waits for them to join us. Then she says, still with her arm on my shoulder, "You've got a lot of attitude. I like that. Attitude and pizzazz. You're trying, putting yourself out there, giving me one hundred percent. Which is good. It means that when I need you to give me one hundred and ten percent, you'll do that, too. Am I right, Eugene?"

"Are you talking about me or her?" he says.

"All three of you." She lets go of my shoulder and perches on a desk. "You guys are so dedicated," she says. "And we don't all have to be vocal soloists do we, Mr. Nik Nak? There are other things I look for. Enthusiasm. Musicality. Reading skills—"

"You know," I tell her, "I can read music. Maybe not as well as some people . . ."

"Excuse me," she says. "You just interrupted me."

I'm starting to detest that *excuse me* of hers!

"I was about to tell you about my concert choir," she tells Eugene. *Eugene?* My ears start to float. "My special elite group. I'm thinking about expanding it. I'll be holding tryouts in a month or so. I'd like you three to audition for me. But before that, we'll be auditioning for the April talent show. You three should try out for that, too."

Oh, right. After she just slapped me down in front of everyone? I can feel my face getting hot again. Then I remember her other words: Celestial. Gorgeous.

"Don't get me wrong, Kira," she says. "I love all my kids. All my kids are special to me. But some," she says, and her eyes are so warm suddenly I have to look away, "are especially special. Kira! Are you listening, or are you still too mad at me? I know you have a lot of pride but . . ."

She thinks I'm special. I am special! I've been waiting for this for so long. I didn't even know I was waiting. I've been waiting and waiting.

"I'm listening," I tell her.

"Good," she says. "I'm telling you about this now, Kira, so you'll have time to work on your reading and counting skills. If you'd like, I'll help you. Concert choir goes till four, sometimes four fifteen, most days, but I'm usually free after that." She walks over to her desk and comes back with some paper. "Here's the information for your parents. It's a major time commitment so I'll need their okay." She goes on and on—about the fabulous shows and trips she's got lined up for concert choir, and the great music, about fund-raising parties and bake sales and dj. dances. I think she says more nice things to Jake, too, and to Eugene. I've stopped listening. I've stopped wondering what I'll sing for the audition, and if Grandma can make it down for the shows, and what I'll wear. I'm looking at the schedule: Extra chorus rehearsal, two thirty to three fifteen every day; concert choir, three fifteen to four; Parent Involvement Night, Tuesday the whatever at seven thirty. I can't do any of it. Not with Tammy breathing down Dad's neck, and Ivan looking for his money. There's no point even mentioning it to Dad. There's no way I can ask him to cut back on his hours.

Eugene starts dancing around the hall the instant we leave. "Oh, I like your attitude, Eugene! I like it so much. And what pizzazz! You three are simply pizzazzling! I'm dazzled!" He turns to Jake. "Oh, wow! Think there's room for a duck in our act? Dirk and the Dazzlers?" He stops and looks at me. I've just crunched up the handout and thrown it in the wastebasket. "Kira! What are you doing?"

"What do you think I'm doing?" I tell him. "I go home right after school, remember? Every day. I have the boys to take care of. I have to babysit a duck. Dad can't come to meetings. I can hardly read music. Should I keep going?"

Jake snorts like Grandma, only more bitterly. I turn and look at him. He looks so angry.

"Why are you looking at me like that?" I say. "You can do it without me. I saw you when Ms. Hill was talking. Any idiot can see you're dying to do it. What?" I shout at him. "You never even sang until a month ago, and now she's telling you how talented you are! You're supposed to be happy!"

"Right." He balls up his handout and chucks it at the basket. It misses. He kicks it and walks off.

"Jake!" I call after him. "You don't need me to do it. You'll try out with Eugene."

He keeps walking.

"What'd I do?" I ask Eugene.

Eugene shakes his head. "It wasn't you. Believe me."

Something about that "it wasn't you" suddenly reminds me of that day at our house. And the way they were talking about the Mighty Mintzmobile before. I look at him. "He's not still grounded?"

Eugene looks down the hall at Jake. "I've gotta get to science."

I grab his arm. "Eugene. What's going on?"

"I can't say," he says. "He'll kill me if I tell you."

The Evil Tongue God

Jake keeps looking at the telephone. *I didn't mean to walk away from you. The reason I can't try out is I'm grounded again. I can't do anything after school. I can't do anything.*

He's lost his phone privileges too. But that's not what's stopping him from calling Kira. It's not even how much he hates the telephone. It's that can of worms again. *You know all those Mondays and Wednesdays I was at lunch with you? Well, guess what. I was supposed to be at speech therapy. And guess what. The Mintzmobile's the speech therapist's friend. And, yes, she called my mom at work again.* No. It was humiliating enough to be sent to speech therapy. But to tell anyone about it? To tell Kira? To say out loud that not only can't he talk, but he's a spineless worm?

"Jake?" His dad knocks on the door. "I'm going for a run. "You feel like coming?"

It's Friday, the day after he learned about the tryouts.

He feels like a worm for not going to school today, too. The three-day President's Day weekend is coming up. He won't see Kira till Tuesday.

Listen. I can't try out. But you have to. If I got myself into chorus, you can find some way to be in the show. And in the concert choir. I know you can.

He can't help himself; his eyes flick to the round glass light fixture on the ceiling. If there was ever anything guaranteed to set off an Evil Tongue God attack, it's wanting to pick up a telephone.

"Jake." His dad knocks again.

It sounds so stupid to him now. Not that he believed his mouth was ruled by a tiny deranged ninja dentist. Except who but the Evil Tongue God could come up with a speech therapist with not just one *B* in her name, but four. "Hi, there, Jake. I'm Barbara Blumberg. You can call me Ms. Blumberg, or Barbara, whichever feels more comfortable." What's stupid, he thinks, is that instead of doing any of the things he wants to do, he's lying here staring at a stupid light fixture.

"Jake." His dad opens the door. "It's bad enough not feeling well. Grounded and sick sort of sounds like overkill, don't you think? I'd say we can unground you long enough for a little run."

His dad doesn't look as angry as he did. Or as

angry as Jake's mom still does. Jake can feel a lump starting in his throat.

"How you feeling now?" his dad says, coming over and standing by the bed.

They both know he's not sick. Jake was astounded his mom let him stay home today.

His dad does a hamstring stretch against the wall, first the right leg, then the left. He grabs his foot and stretches out his quads. Then he reaches down and touches Jake's leg. "A run might help," he says. "Come on. Put some sweats on. Get your sneakers." He walks over to Jake's window and pulls up the shade. "If we, uh, go right now, we might even miss that sleet and freezing rain they're promising."

It's not sleeting yet, but the sky is leaden. The wind off the river cuts right through Jake's fleece as they head for the park. His dad was right, though; fresh air, even damp, chilly air, is good.

"I know you know this," his dad says when Jake stops to tie his shoe. "I just want to say it again, son. There's nothing you can't tell me."

Jake's heart thuds. He wants so badly to tell Dad about Kira, about chorus yesterday, how Ms. Hill praised him. How she wants him to audition. How he wants to do it. He wants to tell him so badly he's afraid to look at him.

They start to run again.

"I, uh, need to make sure you understand some things too," his dad says when it's clear Jake's not going to answer. "You're not grounded for deciding not to go to speech therapy. We'd like to see you try it, but no one can make you. You're grounded for dodging it. For breaking your word to us. For lying again." Jake can feel his dad's eyes boring into him. "We've gone along with everything you wanted. We let you change English teachers. We supported joining chorus. We're doing everything in our power. But you didn't hold up your end of it. That won't do, Jake. It won't even get you what you want."

You think I don't know all that? Jake wants to scream. *Do you think I like being a worm?* It's just that this sick, clammy Clam Boy feeling comes over him even thinking about these speech people with their stuttering journals and video cameras, and recorders, and the mirrors they want him to keep by the telephone, and their talk about "acquainting him with his stuttering behavior," which he is already way, way, way too acquainted with. *I can't do it, Dad. I can't. It feels like torture.*

He wants to tell Dad so badly his throat aches.

They run till an icy rain starts and his father says they have to turn around.

. . .

It rains the rest of the weekend. Jake sorts his comic collection. He pulls his old games and toys out from under his bed and piles them by the door to throw away. He arranges, then rearranges, his models before he decides he's too old for models and adds them to the pile. He calls the time, the weather, Moviefone. He calls directory assistance and when the operator says "What listing please?" he almost keeps himself from hanging up.

He barely leaves his room till Monday lunch, when his mom announces that seeing him in his pajamas for an entire three-day weekend might not be bothering anyone else, but it's truly depressing her, and, after a brief conference with his dad, tells Jake to call Eugene and see if he wants to go downtown to the bookstore and the art supply store. "You're still grounded," she tells him, "but we can certainly permit you to go out and get the materials for Mr. Estrada's English project."

Eugene is spraying bunches of beets with a hose when Jake gets to Kim's Green Farm. "Do you have any idea," he says, pulling off his plastic gloves, "how glad I am to see something that is not a vegetable?"

Jake pulls off his own soggy gloves and, while he wipes his face, checks if Eugene's being sarcastic. He doesn't seem to be. Eugene's mother, behind the counter, gives him a warm smile. His father, who's been neatening the plastic containers above the salad bar, shakes Jake's hand. Even their fat yellow cat stands up from his nest in the onion bin and comes to greet him. He gives the cat a scratch.

"I'm glad to see you too," he tells Eugene.

"In case you were wondering how I'm spending my weekend . . ." Eugene walks to the salad bar. "Here, kitty, kitty!" He holds out a chunk of cuke. "*Psss Psss*. Yo. Wombat. Come here!"

"Eugene!" His mom scolds him in Korean.

"It's not wasting food," he tells her. "He's gonna eat it. Seriously. He loves it. Look at this," he tells Jake as the cat runs over, puts his paws up on Eugene's legs, and licks the cucumber. "He'll fetch it, if I throw it."

"Oh, yeah?" Jake's mood starts to lift.

"Yeah. I'll show you. Radishes bounce better, but he doesn't like them."

"Eugene!" His mom scolds him again.

He drops the cuke on the floor for the cat to eat. Then, while his father's turned away, he grabs two chunks of bread and two pieces of scone from the basket beside the soup kettles and puts them in his pocket. "I'll be back in a few hours," he tells them.

"Be careful," his mom says. Eugene is the only one of the Kims' kids still living at home. The baby of the family. She looks out the window and wrinkles her nose. "Too much rain!" she tells Jake. She points to his feet. "No boots?"

Jake shakes his head. She's so shy about speaking English, he always tells himself he's doing her a favor by not saying much.

While she bends to get something from under the counter, Eugene palms two packs of Nik Naks.

She's too fast for him. And she's got an umbrella in her hand. With another exasperated shake of the head, she bops him with it.

"One was for Jake," he protests, but he puts them back and, with a loud sigh, accepts the umbrella and her kiss.

"So, *qué pasa*?" he asks once they're out the door and walking to the station. "Do I ask what's up, or no?"

"No," Jake says as the umbrella blows inside out.

"You can come under it with me," Eugene says once he's gotten the thing straightened out. It's a dinky one. The spokes are bent. A couple of them stick out at crazy angles.

"No, thanks," Jake says.

"Want to hear about school Friday?" Eugene asks.

"Nope," Jake says.

"No problem," Eugene says. "You didn't miss anything." He has to wrestle the umbrella closed so they can go into the station. "Except lunch with Kira. Don't worry. It wasn't fun. She was in as foul a mood as you are."

By the time the train comes, though, Eugene has managed to get him laughing, imitating two stuck-up girls from Korean school, demonstrating how one got the hiccups in church yesterday, and then the other one caught them from her until it got so loud they had to leave. Jake's never heard of contagious hiccups.

They're still laughing when they get off at Columbus Circle and head downtown. They find the books Mr. Estrada suggested with no trouble. They pick out their poster board and mounting tabs and special glue. Then, even though Jake's not sure why he would go home when he's still got an hour and a half of freedom, they head back to the station.

Eugene has just wrestled his umbrella closed again, and they've just walked down the steps when they hear singing.

Jake's heart leaps. Russell! He must have an amplifier, because Jake doesn't see them.

"What are they doing here?" Eugene says. "She said they weren't playing anymore. She told us they stopped singing."

"I know!" Jake also knows she can't be here. Not with this song Russell's singing. "Here comes Kira, true blue Kira . . ." She'd die before she'd stand there and let her dad sing about her. But he can't help walking faster.

"'Along came Kira, rough, tough Kira'?" Eugene says, hustling to keep up with him. "'Along came Kira and my world turned upside down'? What's up with that?"

Jake nods. "I know!" They follow the sound past the newsstand and the flower seller. They're almost to the ramp when he sees Russell, by himself, sitting on his amp and singing to an empty corridor.

Russell jumps to his feet the minute he sees them. "Hey! Look who's here!" he cries, shaking both boys' hands. "Long time no see! Still raining up there?"

"Oh, yeah," Eugene says. "How's business?"

"Sucks!" Russell says. "They're staying away in droves. I did pretty good on the weekend, but today is, like, forget it. I keep thinking if I haven't got Kira, maybe I should put Dirk in my act."

"Right!" Eugene says before Jake can ask where she is. "Ducky percussion. 'Oh, a bad song is better than no song. Quack! A sad song beats no song at all. Quack! Quack!'"

"Gene, man! I can't believe you remember that song! Wait till I tell Ki! She's upstate this weekend. She took the boys to see their grandma. They went up Friday night."

Eugene gives Jake a quick look then nods at Russell. "Oh, yeah. Right."

So then Eugene knew? And didn't say anything? "Did they take D-D-D- . . . ?"

"After we built him a hundred-dollar duck house?" Russell says. "Hell, no! Plus, I doubt they let ducks on the train."

A homeless man walks over and peers into the guitar case.

"Dream on, buddy," Russell tells him. "Ain't enough in there to bother stealing." He picks up the few coins in the case, and drops them in his pocket. "Maybe you guys should sing with me," he tells Jake and Eugene. "It might change my luck."

He says it so seriously Jake instantly thinks about songs they could sing. But Russell's already glancing at the scattering of wet, grouchy-looking people walking by and shaking his head.

"Nah," he says. "I may as well give it up and go uptown with you guys. In fact, if you're not doing nothing, why don't you come back with me." He laughs. "I made just about enough to get us each a sandwich. You can say hi to Dirk. I'll show you some of the tricks we taught him. Ki should be getting in anytime. My sister's driving them down."

Jake checks the time. He's got more than an hour. "Cool," he says before Eugene can object.

"Excellent!" Russell says. "If there's one thing I don't enjoy, it's coming home to an empty house. By the way," he tells them as he packs the guitar and lifts the amp and microphone and drum machine into the cart. "I'd appreciate if you don't mention this to Ki. I haven't told her I've been playing down here again."

I didn't mean to walk away from you, Jake practices again on the walk from the subway. His pulse races when he sees a female figure huddled at the bottom of Kira's outside steps. The woman is small and thin like Kira. But her hair is long and streaked blond. She's wearing a short leather skirt and high-heeled boots and smoking a cigarette. She's pretty, or would be if she didn't look so tense and sour.

"Tammy!" Russell unlocks the gate, hands Eugene the bag of food, and rushes down the steps. "What are you doing here so early? I want you to meet my good friends, Jake and Gene. Guys!" he calls. "Come say hello to my wife!"

"Ex-," she snaps, not bothering to look at them.

Jake and Eugene give each other a quick glance and stay where they are.

"I been freezing my butt off down here for the last hour," she tells Russell. "Not to mention probably ruined a pair of hundred-dollar boots. Where were you?"

"Out trying to get some money for you, babe," he says. "Like I promised." He looks her over. "You okay?" Jake can hear worry in his voice. "I thought you said you'd be by after six, so you could see the boys."

"That didn't work out," she says. "And what's that supposed to mean, 'trying'?" She looks at Jake and Eugene at the top of the stairs and notices the shopping cart with the equipment. "I thought you said you sold that stuff!"

Jake sees Russell's shoulders tense.

"I know," Russell says.

"You told me it was a done deal," she says. "You said the guy paid you the money. What was that, Russell, more of your—"

The look Russell gives her reminds Jake of himself with Ms. Mintzer. "Tammy, listen," he says. "This ain't a good time for me."

She curses. "When is it? You know, you're not the only one with problems, Russell. I had a real rough week. I've got a lot of stress—"

"I hear you." He holds up his hands, nodding. "I hear what you're saying. Why don't you come on in and sit down, okay? I just picked up some sandwiches."

"I don't need to sit down," she says. "What I need is a beer."

Russell starts to say something, then throws the boys a helpless look. "I apologize, guys," he says opening the door for her. "We'll do this another time. Honest."

"You think that was Kira's mom?" Eugene asks as they head back to the subway. It had stopped raining; it's started again.

"I don't know," Jake says. "And do me a favor. When we see her? Don't ask."

"What was her problem?" Eugene says, getting the umbrella from his backpack.

"I don't know." It was embarrassing to Jake seeing Russell all sheepish and cringing like that.

He's not ready to go home. And he hated Tammy.

"I mean, did you see how her zipper was pinned shut with safety pins?" Eugene says. The catch that holds the umbrella open has broken. The umbrella closes on his head. "And did you check out her teeth?" He opens it again, holding on to the catch so it can't close. "She looks like she sharpens them before she goes to bed at night. She was, like, When Good Barbies Go Bad. And what was that—"

"I should have said we'd sing with him," Jake tells him. "Then we would still b-b-b-be in the station, and T-T-T-Tammy would have given up and left, and when we got there, K-K-K-Kira might have already b-b-b- . . . been home—"

"Oh, right! And you would have gotten home two hours late!" Eugene's so busy being sarcastic he forgets to hang on to the catch. The umbrella collapses again. "This is oh for two, you realize," he says, pushing it up again. "Two visits to Kira's that ended badly. *A*, she wasn't there. *B*, you're assuming she even wants to see you, which, if you ask me, is—"

Jake can feel his throat clenching. "Wh-Wh-Wh-What'd she say to you? What'd you tell her?"

"Nothing!" Eugene sounds offended.

Too offended, Jake thinks. "Are you lying?"

Eugene's voice rises: "Why would I be lying?"

"I don't know. So then what did you talk about at lunch when I wasn't there?"

Eugene shrugs. The umbrella bloops down again. He opens it. "This and that."

"D-D-D-Did she tell you she was going away?"

"She may have mentioned she had plans. I'm not sure. If you'd been at school you'd know."

"And did you say a-a-a-anything to her about me? Or aren't you sure about that, either?"

"No!"

"Well, did she ask?"

"As a matter of fact," Eugene says, "we didn't talk about you."

"Then what'd you talk about?"

"Would you believe, me? She wanted to know about me."

Jake looks into his eyes. "You didn't say anything at all about me?"

"No. I did not reveal any of your precious secrets, if that's what you mean. And why do you keep asking me that?" The umbrella closes yet again.

"'Cause you . . . have this . . . way, Eugene! Of saying the wrong thing at the wrong—"

"What do I say wrong? All I've done all afternoon is go along with you. Go along with you and try to look out for you."

"Yeah? Well, I've already got too many people looking out for me! My mom, my dad, Mintzer!" Alarms are going off in Jake's head, warning him to shut up while he still can. But Eugene looks like such a doofus with the stupid umbrella on his head. "You're all telling me wh-wh-wh-where I have to be, and what I have to do, and what I should be say—"

"Well, maybe you wouldn't need all those people," Eugene says, "if you'd—"

If I'd what? Jake starts to say, but since he doesn't want to hear the answer, he yells, "Shut up!"

"No!" Eugene yells back. "That's all I've done lately is shut up. You said don't tell anyone you're grounded, so I didn't! You didn't want to talk about chorus, and we didn't! You tell me not to talk about Kira, and then when I try not to, you make me, and then you jump all over me!" Jake's never seen him so angry. "I'm sick of you!" Eugene shouts. "Walking around pissed off all the time, telling me what I can and can't say when *you* can't even say—"

Jake doesn't wait to hear if Eugene's actually going to bring up his stutter. "I'll tell you what I'm sick of!" he shouts back. "You and that asinine umbrella!" He grabs it from Eugene, punching the top in, pulling at the bent spokes, ripping the ones he can rip out of their holes, twisting and mashing and smashing the other ones till there's no chance of the umbrella ever opening again. "Shut up, Eugene!" he screams, bashing it on the pavement. "Just shut up!"

"No!" Eugene snatches it away from him. "Everything's a secret, suddenly. You've got secrets. Russell's got secrets. Kira's got secrets. I'm sick of secrets. I don't have any secrets. Not to mention that I can't do anything with you anymore, because you keep getting yourself grounded. Not that I know why I'd want to. I liked you a lot better before she came along!"

"Shut up!" Jake yells again. But this time it's to Eugene's back. Eugene's stalked away.

CHAPTER 21

By the time he gets home, Jake's stopped being mad at Eugene. He just feels bad and stupid.

So, even though he's not sure Eugene will be there, he gets to the bodega twenty minutes early the next morning, stays by the counter till a woman orders a bagel and cream cheese, and then tells the counterman, "Same for me." Then, while he stands outside, stamping his feet against the bitter cold, jingling the change in his pocket, he practices his *B*s. He's promised his parents he'll go to see Ms. Blumberg today. What he hasn't told them is what he's planning to say. He's come up with a test for himself. It won't unground him or get his privileges back. No one will even know. He doesn't care. If he can get out three or more *B*s, it will prove that he's not dodging anything. He's not running away. He's not a spineless worm who's afraid to face a speech therapist. He doesn't need speech therapy.

Eugene's eyes are guarded as he rounds the corner.

"Hey." Jake holds out the bag. "I . . ."—he closes his lips to form the *B* and begs them to open—"bought you a . . . bagel." The *B*s puff out glitchlessly. It feels like a good sign.

He can see Eugene trying to decide if he's too angry to take it.

"It's not your usual," he tells him. Eugene's been on a cinnamon raisin kick lately. The woman also ordered a large coffee. "It's an everything. And I got you some c-c-c- . . . offee. R-R-R- . . . egular. I wasn't sure if th-th-th-that means it has sugar, so I gr-gr-gr-grabbed some extra." It's coming apart now, but after the *B*s he hardly cares.

"Thank you," Eugene says, taking the bag from him. "I was just thinking I should think about drinking coffee."

"Really?" Jake wonders if Eugene has any idea how happy he is to see him. Now he wishes he'd bought him some Nik Naks, too. And a new umbrella. He waits eagerly as Eugene opens the bag and unwraps the bagel and does his cream-cheese-scraping routine.

"Looks like a good bagel," Eugene says, taking a bite. "Mmm." He nods, then pulls off the little tab in the top of the coffee container and tilts it to his lips. "*Eeew!* People drink this?" he says, squinching his face. "It's like drain cleaner!"

Kira walks up to them. "I'll drink it if you don't want it," she tells him.

He passes it to her. "Be my guest! Jake bought it for me. Worst case, it'll keep your hands warm."

"Yeah. I wish the sun would come out." She gives Jake a hesitant hello nod. "How's it goin'?"

He glances at Eugene. "Uh . . ."

She tries the coffee. "Yick!" she tells Eugene. "You're right!"

"Y-Y-Y-You don't h-h-h-have to drink it," Jake tells her.

"I do if I want to stay awake," she says, taking another sip. "I got, like, three hours' sleep."

"You got back late?" Eugene asks her.

"How'd you know I went somewhere?" she asks suspiciously.

"Uh . . ." Eugene hesitates, but only for an instant. "We called you," he says, taking both Kira and Jake by surprise.

"You did?" she says. "What for?"

Jake doesn't wait to hear what he'll come up with. "J-J-J-Just . . . you know . . . a fr-fr-fr-friendly hi."

"I could've used a friendly hi," she says.

"So, how was it up there, upstate?" Eugene asks. "Was it fun?"

She shrugs. "It was okay. There was a ton of snow. How 'bout you?"

Jake nods. "Okay, I guess."

"So was I cool enough?" Eugene asks once they've left her and all agreed to meet at lunch. "I didn't say anything I wasn't supposed to?" There's still an edge to his voice but Jake can feel Eugene wanting things to be okay between them.

"Yeah. No." He nods. "You were cool. You were very cool. Thanks," he adds.

Then he goes back to his Blumberg prep, his goal being to dash up there after fourth period, get in, get out, and meet Kira and Eugene at the lunch table. If he passes this test, the whole Blumberg thing should only take two minutes.

Jake's heart feels like it's taking up all the room in his chest.

"Jake!" Ms. Blumberg smiles when he opens her office door. "How nice to see you."

He can't help glancing at her light fixture. Fluorescent. That's a good sign.

He commands himself to breathe. "Hey," he says. "Barbara!"

He decided on that third period, decided *Ba* was a safer bet than *Bl*.

Two down. He manages a smile.

She nods toward the chair across from her. "Have a seat. Did you bring your lunch?"

He stays by the door. "Actually . . ." There was no "actually" in his script. His throat clenches. He commands himself to breathe again. "I just came . . . by . . ." The "by" is way too loud. He sounds like an android. *But that was three! He did it! Should he try for another?* "To say . . . good . . . bye." *Yes!* "Because . . ." *Unbelievable!* "I . . . think . . . I'm . . . doing . . . okay . . . on my own."

"I'm happy to hear it," she says. "I'm pleased you stopped by to tell me. And remember, anytime you change your mind about doing it on your own, I'm here."

She's happy? He feels as if he's lost fifty pounds! He practically dances out her door. He takes the steps to the lunchroom two at a time. *No cowardly spineless wimpy dodger would have dared go for five. I was right!* he tells himself. *I can do anything I want when I put my mind to it. I don't need Barbara Blumberg!*

"I've always wondered how far up the state you have to go before you're upstate," Eugene is saying when Jake brings his tray over to their table. "What'd you guys do up there?"

"Not that much," Kira says, giving Jake a quick

wave. "You know. Lay around, ate, visited people. How 'bout you?"

Eugene conspicuously doesn't look at Jake. "Lay around. Ate. Visited a few people. So, was it fun?"

She picks up a chicken nugget. "It was all right."

Jake bites open a ketchup packet and squeezes it on his burger. If only he could tell them how brilliantly he did. How masterfully he handled Barbara Blumberg!

"But you didn't have a good time?" Eugene asks.

"No, it was fine," she says. "I mean, Grandma took us to work with her Saturday so everyone could fuss over the boys, and this man, Mr. Corrigan, who's one of the residents, but he's not like some of the others—he can walk and do everything—he gave me a lesson on the organ."

"Cool!" Jake says. For a school lunch burger, his tastes almost good today. He eats it in three mouthfuls.

"And the boys loved it because Aunt Phyllis gave them all my cousins' stuffed dinosaurs, so now they can sleep surrounded by meat eaters. And Sunday we went to church and everyone was, like, 'Oh, Kira, you look so New York. I hardly recognized you with your short hair and your feather boa."

Eugene raises his eyebrows. "You wore that feather thing to church?"

"Yeah," she says. "And then my aunt and uncle and everyone came for lunch, and we took the boys tobogganing and made a snowman. And Monday I got to see my friends, which was . . . I don't know . . . a little weird."

"Then what happened?" Jake asks because she's got that tense look again.

She rolls her eyes. "Then my aunt drove us back Monday afternoon, and she'd never driven down to the city before, and traffic was jammed up and she missed her exit, and I tried to call Dad for directions, and he wasn't answering the phone, and then we get there and there's no Dad."

Jake and Eugene look at each other.

"And his cell phone wasn't answering, and Aunt Phyllis is, like, 'I can't stay here all evening! I've gotta get back! But I can't leave you here alone!' And she hadn't seen the apartment before, and she didn't think much of it—big surprise!—and then she was gonna fix us all dinner, and there was nothing to make"—Kira's voice is rising—"and of course by then she's so freaked she wanted to take us all home with her, but I said no because I was worried about Dad, and then when he did finally get back, at, like, ten something, they had a gigantic screaming fight, and she was, like, 'Where were you? You are not a fit parent!' And he's, like, 'What? I was working. I forgot to charge up the phone. You didn't have to stay. Kira would have handled it. Kira's used to staying with the kids alone.' Which of course set her off again. And then when she finally left, he was in a giant funk, and when I asked him what was up, because he wasn't supposed to be at work, he wouldn't say." She looks from Jake to Eugene and back to Jake. "Why am I telling you this, right? Way more than you wanted to know."

"No." Jake says. "No. I had a cr-cr-cr-crappy weekend too. I was in a f-f-f- . . . terrible mood. Eugene can tell you."

"Yeah." Eugene nods. "He mutilated my umbrella."

Jake watches her try to figure out if Eugene's joking.

"First he strangled it," Eugene says. "Then he dismembered it. It was ugly."

Kira gives Jake a long look. "I know the feeling."

She's waiting for them outside the door after school. "I'm gonna go get some more coffee," she says.

"Uh," Eugene says. "I'm not sure I'm a coffee

person. No offense, Jake. It was an excellent bagel."

"I'll come," Jake says instantly, even though he's grounded and supposed to be going directly home. "I didn't get much sleep last night either."

"I guess I'll come too," Eugene says.

"So, what was up with you?" Kira asks Jake once she's ordered their coffees and they're standing in the cold outside the bodega saying how gross it tastes.

He avoids her eyes. "Just . . . y-y-y-you know. The usual."

"You're not gonna tell me?" she says. "I'd love to hear about someone's life that's more messed up than my own." She makes a face. "Sorry! I didn't mean that the way it sounds."

"No." Jake nods. "I know what you're saying. M-M-M- . . . isery loves c-c-c- . . . ompany, right?"

"Right," she says.

He's not sure if she's noticed they both said "love." Or if Eugene did. Maybe it's not why she's got that weird look on her face, or why they all immediately go back to saying how this coffee really does taste like drain cleaner, and "When was the last time you tried drain cleaner?" and "You can see why they invented the frappuccino." It's why Jake's face is red.

"Dreams and Baloney"

He likes me! It's like a hum I can almost hear, or a glow I can feel glowing right through Eugene. Which is what's so weird about it. I can't tell if he's deliberately started not sitting next to me at lunch, not standing next to me when we're outside, or if Eugene deliberately is. Now, for example. We just walked into the auditorium side by side, Jake, me, and Eugene; yet somehow, as we sat down, it became Jake, Eugene, and me.

"You'll be happy to hear I'm in an excellent mood today!" Ms. Hill announces. "Let's talk about the talent show."

"Let's not," I lean across Eugene to tell Jake.

He gives me a quick "I know what you mean" look, but I can't tell if he's talking about himself or me.

"Night of a Thousand Stars," she says. "Tryouts March eighth." She's wearing a rusty-orange velvet scarf today, long as my feather thing, and a long vest made out of some African material, and one of those huge-collared cowl necks, and her billowy pants. And of course the earrings. She wouldn't be Ms. Hill without her giant silver earrings. She paces back and forth in front of us, stopping only long enough to look in people's faces. "That's three weeks from tomorrow, Maya. Friday. Eleven fifty. It's early dismissal that day, April, so do not make other plans. And I know how much you like your lunch, Felipe, so if you want it before, say, two o'clock, bring it, because you'll be here a long time. There's a lot of talent in this room. And don't think I'm only talking to my eighth graders, Bryan," she tells the other skinny sixth grader.

"Me?" he says in a stupid voice.

"Why not? You're in chorus aren't you?" She looks up at all of us. "Why do you think the show's called Night of a Thousand Stars, people? Because you're all my stars! You think that sounds corny, but I mean it. Just taking that chance and getting up on that stage to try out makes you a star." She's moving to the end of the row now, walking up the aisle.

She stops in front of us and smiles right at me.

I need to tell her I can't do this.

"That's right," she says. "I'm talking to you new people, as well, and you shy types who've never been on stage before and don't know what a kick it can be. Take a chance, shy types! If you're not a soloist, form a group. You never know. You might surprise yourself." She smiles at all of us.

I so much don't want to tell her!

"Yo! Ms. Hill!" someone calls out. "Can me and Desiree sing a duet?"

"Excuse me?" Ms. Hill tucks her chin in and puts her hands on her hips. "Excuse me? Where are your manners? And it's 'Desiree and I.' And, yes, you can do a duet."

"Can Tondra and I do a dance?" someone else calls.

"What'd I just say?" she says. "If you have a question, raise your hand! Yes, you can do a dance."

Hands shoot up all over the room.

"I write raps," Bryan says. "Can I do a rap? Could I do two?"

"I'm taking harp lessons," someone else says. "Can I bring in my harp?"

"Can my family come?"

"To the show, absolutely," she says. "Tryouts are just for us. You can dance, or read a poem, or play the harp, or the French horn, or anything else, as long as you follow my ground rules: No rudeness. No crudeness. No negativity. We show respect for our fellow performers and for ourselves. We do not make anyone feel small. We keep our acts under five minutes. I don't want any parents or grandparents or aunts and uncles dying of old age while you guys are on the stage. And if you bring her the sheet music, Ms. Bolden will accompany you. Any more questions?"

Eugene's hand goes up.

"What are you asking?" I whisper, checking Jake's face. Maybe he and Eugene are doing something and didn't tell me.

"Eugene?" Ms. Hill says. "You had a question?"

"No." He shakes his head. "No question."

"I have one," one of the other boys calls out. "What if you want to be in it, but you have no talent?"

"Felipe," she says as everyone starts laughing. "I'm not even going to dignify that with an answer."

"No," he says. "I'm serious. Could you, like, put on silver body makeup and be a statue like that—"

"Felipe," she says, "you can't hold still for thirty seconds. Does anyone else have a *serious* question?"

Eugene raises his hand again. "Uh . . . what if we don't know yet if we want to be in it? I mean, do we need to decide now?"

"The sign-up sheet will be on the piano after rehearsal," she tells everyone. "If you have the slightest urge to perform, put your name down. Don't even worry about whether you're good enough. Just get your act together and try it on us. You'll never know unless you try."

Eugene's hand goes up again. I can't tell if Jake looks worried or just puzzled.

"No more questions!" Ms. Hill says. "Anyone with more questions, see me afterward. Stand up, everyone! Mouths open! Hands out of your pockets! Ladies in the back, your mouths should be as open as mine! The more open your mouth is, the more sound will come out. You think I'm joking?" She drops her jaw and makes a sound so beautiful it makes my heart hurt. "An A please, Ms. Bolden . . ."

"What were you gonna ask?" I whisper as Ms. Bolden plays a chord.

Eugene shrugs. "Just about the concert choir. When those tryouts are."

Concert choir? You? I almost say, but Jake's already saying, "Why, Eugene? You know we're not trying out for anything."

I lean across Eugene again. "You really can't?"

"No!" Jake snaps.

"No need to bite my head off," I snap back.

"Eugene!" Ms. Hill calls. "Remind your friends what happens to people who are rude enough to talk during rehearsal."

"Out on their ear?" he says.

"Thank you," she says. "Ms. Bolden, another A, if you don't mind."

We go through the exercises and then on to the songs. We're mostly working on gospel songs; it's Black History month. "Beautiful, Michelle!" she calls out. "I can see you're getting that pretty voice of yours loosened up for the tryouts. Felipe, what do you mean you have no talent? Yeah, Jake, sing it to me! You know, you guys are getting me excited. Nice, Kira! See what I mean about letting your mouth open?" She gives Ms. Bolden one of those big, shining smiles. "Don't they sound good today, Ms. Bolden? This excitement is contagious!"

We do sound amazingly good today. There's this one song, "People Get Ready," that I really, really love. She's right about dropping my jaw. It makes a huge difference. I just wish she'd stop looking so proud of me. It's bad enough I can't try out without her making it harder.

As soon as rehearsal's over everyone starts rushing around, forming into clumps, talking a mile a minute about what they're going to do. There's a big line by the piano. I'm amazed how many people are signing up.

One nice thing: At least when Eugene gets up to leave, I can move over next to Jake. I can feel that humming, glowing thing again between us. We stand there in the aisle, not saying anything, but not going

anywhere either. I'm not sure what he's thinking. I'm
thinking if I had any guts at all I'd walk up to Ms. Hill
and be done with it, so I can stop feeling all weird and
pissed and sad, and she'll stop giving me those looks.

I can't get myself to go over to her.

"Kira!" I jump as Jake touches my arm. He nods
toward the piano. Eugene's joined the line of kids
waiting to sign up.

"Uh, Eugene? What are you doing?" Jake asks
when we go over to him.

"Putting my name down," Eugene says, trying
hard to be all casual and matter-of-fact.

"Well, forget it," I tell him. "You can sign us up
all you want. We still can't do it."

"I know that," he says. Not huffy, but not pre-
tending to be casual anymore either.

Jake and I look at each other. Eugene has a voice
like a foghorn. As far as I know he doesn't play an
instrument. And the thought of him dancing . . .
This is a joke, right? I want to say. *I'm the singer
here. Jake and I are the singers.*

"So . . . then . . . what would you . . . do?" I force
myself to ask.

"I haven't decided yet," he says. "All I know is it's
a talent show, and Ms. Hill said I have talent." He
looks Jake square in the eye. "So I'm signing up."

CHAPTER 23

Whatever Eugene's so-called talent is, he won't tell us. I ask him a bunch of times over the next week. Then I drop it. Jake, in one of our few Eugene-less moments, has told me to ease up. He says Eugene's upset that everyone except him has secrets.

"I'll give him some of mine," I tell Jake. "He can have all of them. He can take some of my problems, too, while he's at it. He's welcome to them."

Money and Tammy. Those are the two biggies at the moment.

I've already tucked the boys in with their dinosaurs the night Tammy shows up. I'm lying on the couch getting mentally prepared to start looking at my science notes for tomorrow's test when I hear her knocking on the gate.

"Russell, honey?" she calls. "Are you in there? Russell? I need to talk to you. Come on, baby! Let me in. It's cold out here."

I tiptoe over to the window. I push back the curtain and peek out through the bars. She's got on a short fur jacket and a leather miniskirt. She's standing under the outside light, holding up a mirror, fixing her makeup—first mascara, then lip pencil. Whatever anyone thinks of her, Tammy is beautiful. Even though I can almost hear Grandma saying, "Curiosity killed the cat," I open the window a few inches. "Hey, Tammy," I say. "He's not here. He's working."

"Oh, Kira, honey, am I glad to see you!" she says. "I've been out running around all day. I need a bathroom real bad."

She looks so shivery and pitiful I almost go to the door. Then I think, *Russell, Baby? Kira, Honey? That ought to sound friendly. Why doesn't it?*

"Come on," she says. "Let me in, Kira. I need to pee."

That could be why she's so jumpy. I'm getting a weird feeling, though. Now that she's fully turned toward me, there's something off here. Her hair's kind of greasy-looking. She hasn't done too neat a job with the mascara. Her tights have a hole above the knee. I'm remembering a bunch of times this past week when I picked up the phone and no one said hello back. I'm thinking maybe it wasn't Jake, the way I hoped. I think about Grandma telling me, "She's okay when she's okay," and change to my Grandma at Pine Manor voice. "He's at work, Tammy."

She curses. "You expect me to believe that? He ain't at work. He's back there in the bedroom. Hiding, per usual. Just tell me: Did he sell the stuff or not? Has he got the money?"

Her voice is so shrill that even though there are two doors between me and her, I check to make sure the chain lock's on.

"What stuff? What money?" It seems like the more Dad gives her, the more she wants from him, and the more he gives her, the more hours he has to work. And I know he's been giving it to her. I've gone with him to get the money orders. "I don't know what you're talking about, Tammy."

"Yeah, you do," she says. "The music stuff. Guitars, keyboards, drums kit, amps. The whole nine yards. Go tell him if he won't sell it, I'll do it for him. I got a guy who'll pay me cash. No. Never mind. I'll tell him! Russell!" She leans over and yells into the window, calling him a bunch of names.

"Shhh! Quiet!" I tell her. "You'll wake the boys!"

"They're my boys!" she shouts. "I can wake them any time I want. It's my apartment! I'm their mom, not you. Chris, Charlie! Mommy's here! Come let me in!"

I run over and put the TV on real loud. Then I go back and make sure their door is still closed. I open it and peek in. They're both in bed.

"Ki!" Chris's voice sounds tiny. "Who is it?"

"Nobody." I shut the door behind me and go over to him. Charlie's still asleep. "Just somebody who wanted to use the bathroom."

I wouldn't believe me, but he seems to. "Who?" He sounds scared.

"Just . . . someone," I say as I tuck him in again. "A loud, not-nice person. I'll make her go away and then I'll come back in."

"Take Velocy," he says, handing me the biggest dinosaur.

I feel like climbing into bed with him. It's like that time in the subway, when Dad went off to get us lunch and it was just me and the boys and some old disgusting drunk started coming on to me and I just had to handle it. Till Dad got back.

I run and get the phone, and call Dad.

"Tammy's outside," I tell him. "She's going nuts. Where are you?"

He curses. "On my way to the airport. Let me talk to her."

"Uh-uh! I'm not opening the door!"

"No. I know. Pass her the phone out the window. And whatever you do, don't raise your voice to her. It'll just set her off."

"Thanks for telling me that now!"

I carry the phone back to the living room so he can hear her yelling in the window: "Chris, Charlie! Mommy's here. Come see Mommy! Mommy loves you!"

He curses again.

"Tammy"—I fight to keep my voice under control—"my dad wants to talk to you."

"Forget Russell!" she shouts. "Russell's nothin'. He's less than nothin'. Just give me my stuff. And let me see my babies. I want my babies!"

"You can't see them," I tell her. "And you can't take anything." I don't bother to remind her she'd need a hand truck and a van to get it all out of here. But I can't resist adding, "It's not yours, anyway. It's his!"

"Oh, yeah?" she screams. "And who are you? Russell's wife? That would be me, in case you forgot. Mrs. Russell Stickles. There's community property in New York State. What's his is mine!" And then her eyes change. "Listen, Kira. I don't suppose you've got a few bucks I could have. Just till tomorrow."

"Excuse me?" *She's asking me for money?* My ears

start to float. "Excuse me?" *Next thing she'll be asking Chris and Charlie for money!* "Excuse me?" *There's got to be something less lame I can think of to say!*

My mind jumps to Ms. Hill and her Excuse Me of Death. "Excuse me." I force myself to stop screaming. "Excuse me." I force myself to breathe. "So, if what's his is yours"—the hand that isn't holding the phone clutches the velociraptor—"are you here for the kids? Because if you want them, Tammy, go on and take them! I've got a lot of things I could do with my life if I didn't have to cook dinner and clean and look after them all the time. In fact, if you want, I'll pack their bags right now. What do you say, Tammy? Do you want them?"

My heart is thudding. What if she says yes? What will I do then?

There's a giant silence. She's stopped yelling. "I'd take them if I could, Kira. You know I would. It's just, you know, I've got some problems."

She says it as if I'm supposed to feel sorry for her.

"You think I don't have problems? We've all got problems. Dad's got problems. Your kids have problems." *It's a miracle they aren't running out right now to see what's going on.* "And you know their biggest problem, Tammy? You! When was the last time you called them, or took them anywhere, or sent a birthday present, or a card, or anything? And now you think you're going to walk in here and screw things up even more? No. Go away, Tammy. You're not coming in here. No one needs you here. Leave. It's what you do the best!"

I can't believe how in control my voice sounds. In my guts, though, I can feel myself screaming at my own mom.

I don't stop shaking till Tammy's up the stairs and I hear the gate slam.

"Ki?" Dad calls. "Ki, is she gone? Ki? Are you okay?"

I've forgotten the phone.

"Yeah." I check the clock. It's not even eight yet. I'd have guessed midnight. "Where are you, Dad?"

"On my way home," he says. "Just leaving the terminal. Want me to stay on with you till I get there?"

"No," I tell him. "I'm okay."

I take the phone to the bathroom, set it down on the toilet, splash cold water on my face, and brush my teeth. Then I call a number I know by heart even though I've never called it before.

Jake's father answers. "I'm sorry," he tells me. "Jake can't come to the phone."

No! I refuse to let Tammy make me cry.

I go in and lie down on the floor between the boys' beds with the phone in my hand and wait for Dad.

CHAPTER 24

Dad's face is grim when he walks in. "Get your coat!" he says. "I'm double-parked. I told my fare this was on the way. I doubt he believes me." He leans over the boys' beds and pats them awake. "Come on, guys. We're going for a ride. Ki, help me out here." We stuff their arms into their jackets over their pajamas, grab up pillows and meat-eaters, and hustle them, confused and whimpering, to the cab. I'm so glad that someone's telling me what to do I don't ask why, or where we're going.

"Small family emergency," he tells the man as he buckles the boys in the backseat next to him. "We'll take the highway down. We'll get you to Brooklyn in no time."

I climb in front with him.

What are you thinking? I want to ask him as he drives, stony-faced. *What's going to happen to us?* I keep wondering where my mom lives. Not that she's ever been any help. She could be as bad as Tammy. There's also my homework to worry about, and tomorrow's science test, and Dirk, whom I left outside in the freezing cold. *This is no way to live,* I want to tell him. *I'm sick of it! She's your wife, Dad. Why should I have to figure out if she has to pee or not?* Round and round I go, telling off Tammy, telling off Dad, telling my mom off, worrying.

When the man gets out, a woman in a fur coat climbs in. "Oh, look at this!" she says. "How sweet. The whole family taking a ride with Daddy." She wants to know our names and how old we are, and if it's fun going to work with Daddy. Her perfume smells up the cab. The only good thing is that by the time she leaves, I'm annoyed enough to stop feeling like I'm going to cry.

We pick up more people. We drop them off. Dad explains to all of them that we're his kids. Some ask a question or two but most just go, "Oh, yeah?" and then pick up their cell phones or go back to their thoughts.

We drive all over the city. I keep glancing back at Chris and Charlie. Charlie's eyes are glazed as he spins his pacifier in his mouth. Chris is asleep, clutching Velocy. I keep replaying what I said to Tammy, how I said I could have a life if I didn't have them to take care of. I meant it. Which scares me.

Except for now and then asking how I'm doing,

or apologizing for stopping short, or cursing out other drivers, Dad just sits there with that grim look on his face and drives, which scares me too.

At some point a man in a tuxedo holding a cello case waves us down. "Carnegie Hall," Dad tells me as he stops for him and pops the trunk. "Concert must be getting out."

It feels like the first thing he's said in hours.

"You know, I used to be a musician too," he tells the man with a bitter laugh as soon as he gets in. They chat a little as we make our way through traffic. By the time we get to a bridge, they've stopped talking. Dad turns on the radio. Wherever we are now, it's way quieter on this side of the river than in Manhattan. I'm starting to like riding around in the dark like this, just riding around, looking at the lights, not knowing where we are. I kick off my sneakers, reach back for one of the stuffed dinosaurs, and lean it against the window like a pillow. Sitting here like this with the heat turned up, jazz playing real low, I can almost pretend the rest of tonight never happened.

We let the man out at a little house on a street that looks more like upstate than New York City. Then we drive back to a highway and Dad pulls in at a diner.

"I'm just gonna run in for a sec," he says. "Want anything?"

I shake my head. If it were up to me, I'd stay in here forever.

He makes sure all our doors are locked and goes inside. I sit there staring at the neon sign. *Flushing Diner.*

"I hope the food's better than the name," I say when he gets back. I haven't said anything in so long my voice sounds like a little old Pine Manor lady. "That's the worst name I ever heard."

"Because we're in Flushing," he says, handing me a can of soda. "We might as well go back out to the airport now, long as we're in Queens. Pick up a fare."

"Why would somebody name a place Flushing?" I say.

He pulls the tab on his soda. It comes off in his hand. "Figures," he says and puts the can back in the bag.

"Where do you go when your life is down the tubes?" I say. "Flushing. Flushing, drain capital of the world." *I've been hanging out with Eugene for too long.*

My straw's making straw noises on the bottom of the can when he says, "I could tell you I'm sorry

I ever got you down here to the city, Ki, but I'd be lying. I'm sorry about a lot of things in my life," he says. "Not about that."

I try to think of another Flushing joke. Nothing comes to mind.

"Ki," he says. "If you want to pack it in, I won't fight you."

Is this what he's been thinking about all night? I stop breathing. "What do you mean, pack it in? You mean, go back to Grandma?" With all the things I've thought about—murdering Tammy, beating up Dad, beating myself up for ever getting off that stupid couch—leaving wasn't one.

"Phyllis and Ma have been after me for weeks now," he says, looking straight ahead, out the window. "Asking me why I'm putting everyone through this, telling me how you're too skinny, and the boys are too skinny, and your color is bad because you don't get any fresh air. They been telling me how there's this new community chorus, with some hot-shot choral person from some college or other. They say it's as good as the one you're in. Mr. Corrigan's offering to give you free piano lessons. They also said something about some big, new, fancy supermarket going up. They say it'll be hiring. I wouldn't have to work nights. We could find someplace to live where the boys could run around outside and go to preschool." He sits there while the blood pounds in my ears. "You're not saying anything, Ki."

I don't dare look at him. "Are you saying we'd all leave?" It sounds so good to me. It sounds so easy.

"I'm putting it out there," he says. "Think about it: No more fun-filled times with Tammy throwing fits on the doorstep, scaring you half to death, no being alone with the boys every night eating frozen pot pies. No having to do everything and solve everything and take care of everything, including your old man. Back to your old life, your old friends . . ."

My mind jumps to that day in the subway, with the cops. If he'd offered me the choice then, I'd have leaped at it. But then I'd never have . . .

"I have a life here, Dad," I tell him.

"Yeah." He laughs that bitter laugh again. "You have a life. It just sucks, is all."

"It doesn't *totally* suck," I say.

At first I think I'm only talking about Jake. And Ms. Hill. And Eugene. Then it hits me: Dad's just said he knows what it's like for me. He's saying he'd go back to boony land and bag groceries to make it better. He's saying he'd turn his whole life upside down to be with me. I slide over and put my arms around his neck. "It doesn't all suck, Dad. You don't suck."

"Ki," he says, "that's the nicest thing you ever said to me."

It's weird. He's put his arms around me lots of times. But mine around him? When was the last time that happened? The day I got here?

We stay there like that, not moving, not saying anything.

"Dad?" I ask him into his shoulder. "Was my mom like Tammy?"

"No, Kira," he says. "Your mom was a lot like you. Your mom was great."

CHAPTER 25

"Are you saying you're ready to keep on like this?" he asks once I've gone back to my own side of the seat.

It's awhile before I can talk. "On," I say. "Just not like this."

"So then what are we gonna do about it?" he says. "I mean, there's one thing I can do right away, besides talking to Tammy, which there's no point even trying until she cools down, and changing the lock on the outside gate, which I should have done months ago. I'll sell the instruments. They're not doing me a lot of good. That'll get her off our back for a while. What else?" He looks serious.

I have a whole laundry list of things. But it feels so good not being mad at him that I'm scared to rock the boat. So I start with something small: "You could teach me to read music. I could use some help with it."

"Help with music?" His laugh rings out. "That's an easy one! That I can definitely do. I'll teach you anytime you want. But where'd that come from?"

I tell him about concert choir. I tell him what Ms. Hill said to me.

He sits back and looks at me. "I can't believe you didn't tell me!"

"Why?" I say. "There was no point. Since I can't be in it. They rehearse after school. When they get close to their concerts they rehearse every day."

"Whoa, there." He holds his hand up. "Slow down. When's the audition?"

"I don't know yet. She hasn't said. I think in a few weeks."

"A few weeks? I can teach you in a few days! You can say anything you want about me, but Russell Stickles knows—"

"I can read the notes," I tell him. "Mr. Corrigan taught me. The lines in the treble are Every Good Boy Does Fine. And the spaces in the bass are All Cows Eat Grass. But I don't get how you can look at a bunch of notes on the page and know how you sing it. I mean, I'm still figuring out the first ones, and everyone else is already halfway down the page."

Dad's nodding. "I know how that is. But it's kind of hard to work on that in the dark. How's your counting? She won't care how great your voice is if you come in wrong."

"I don't always . . . ," I start to say.

He looks at me. "Hit the nail on the head, huh? So then let's work on your counting." He reaches across to the glove box and pulls out a flashlight.

"Now?" I say as he rummages for a pad and takes the pen from the clipboard on the seat between us. "I thought we were going to the airport so we could make some money."

"We are," he says. "But first we're taking a music break. You'll never get in that group if you can't count."

"I can't be in it anyway," I remind him. "You have to be at work. I mean, even if we could get someone to stay with the boys one time, so I could do the audition . . ."

"Ki." He puts his hand on my arm. "You told me you wanted help with your music. I can help you with it. So let me help."

"What are we gonna do, get Tammy to babysit?"

"Hey. One step at a time here, okay? Speaking of which, you know about time signatures? Like three/four and four/four and six/eight? And note values?"

"A little," I tell him.

"Fine. We don't even need paper to do that." He switches off the flashlight. "Four/four means there are four beats to the measure, right?" he says, drumming four beats on the steering wheel. "A quarter note gets one beat. You know what a quarter note looks like?"

"Yes. It's one of those filled-in guys on a stick."

"With a tail, or without?"

"Without," I say. "The ones with the tails are the eighths."

"Right. And it's called an eighth note why?"

"Because they're a half of a quarter? And there are eight of them in a measure?"

"Only if you're in four/four," he says. "What about if you're in three/four?"

"Is this music or arithmetic?" I ask him.

"Don't get smart with me, Ms. Stickles. 'Amazing Grace.' Would you say that's in three or in four? Beat it out for me. I'll give you a clue. When you start on the last beat of a measure, that's called a pickup. Or an upbeat."

"Okay. Then it starts on three. Three, one, two, three—"

"Bingo! Now do you know about dotted quarters?"

We go through a bunch of songs like that. I'm getting it! We keep going till my bladder can't take it anymore. Then I run into the diner. There are only a few cars in the parking lot now. It's twenty past one. My color, at least in the Flushing Diner ladies room mirror, *is* fairly horrible. My skin tone reminds me of overcooked cabbage. But I blame that completely on Tammy. And I don't think I'm any thinner than when I moved down. And my hair is way cooler. I wonder why I never asked Dad to teach me music before.

"Why'd you tell that cellist person you *used* to be a musician?" I tell him when I get back to the car. "You're a good musician," I say, unpacking the doughnuts and coffee I bought on the way out. "And a great teacher."

"I'm glad you said that, Ki," he says. "Because I just had an idea. For how you can get to those rehearsals."

"Seriously?" I unwrap a glazed doughnut. It looks like someone sat on it, but it tastes delicious.

"There's this woman upstairs in 6-D," he says. "Ms. Charles?" It's too dark to see his eyes sparkling, but I know they are. "She's a retired kindergarten teacher. Every time I go to her floor to pick up the garbage, she opens her door. Which says she either thinks I'm cute, or she hasn't got enough to do. Plus, she's always stopping on the street to talk to the boys. So, here's what I'm thinking: Nice old lady? Teaching background? Seems like a babysitter to me! I know," he says. "It sounds a little sketchy. But you don't know unless you ask, right? She might not charge that much for a couple of hours. She might even do it for free. But now here's the best part," he says, biting into his doughnut. "Her son-in-law works for a record producer. I can't remember which label. One of the big ones. So I'm thinking, maybe I don't rush out and sell the instruments. This could be, like, two birds with one stone, right? A sitter for your life. A chance for mine. I've got a couple of new song ideas. They feel like they could be my best ones yet. Plus, if we're really gonna get your reading up to speed for that audition, we're gonna need the keyboards. At the very least. So I don't know about you, Ki. I can't see selling them."

My heart started sinking the instant he said, "Here's the best part." All I can think of is Grandma going, "If something feels too good to be true, it probably is."

"Oh, Dad," I say.

"What?" He puts his coffee down. "Why are you sighing? You're looking at me like, there he goes again."

"Because there you go again." He's trying. He's trying so hard. And he's so nice to me. But he's still Dad. And everything's still so complicated.

"I gotta keep dreaming, Ki," he says. "It's gotten me this far. It's gotten me you." Before I can say, "Yeah, but where do dreams stop and baloney begin? How do you tell the difference between dreams and baloney?" he starts drumming on the steering wheel. "You know that song, 'We've Come This Far by Faith'? Come on now. Stay with me here." He beats out a rhythm. "Buh-BAH-uh, BAH-uh, BAH-uh-bah-bah. . . . How would you count that?"

Kira and Jake

It's still dark when the phone rings that morning. Jake reaches a hand out of the covers and grabs it before his mom can pick up in her bedroom. Just because Kira tried him last night, there's no reason to think it's Kira again, but . . .

"You wouldn't believe what's been going on," she says.

Jake looks up at the ceiling and takes a deep breath. "T-T-T-Tell me."

The story pours out of her—about Tammy showing up and Kira's Excuse Me of Death, about Russell roaring in to get them and then offering to move back to Claryville, about driving all the way to the apartment at two a.m. to make sure Dirk hadn't frozen, and writing scales on the back of trip sheets in the parking lot of the Flushing Diner.

Jake is trying to untangle his tongue to say that he's met Tammy, and he hated her too, when Kira says, "I need to see you. Can you meet me before school?"

· · ·

Jake gets to the bodega so early that the schoolyard is empty. The streetlights are still on. The only people in the store are the Tasty Kake man and Kira.

"I need the biggest cup of coffee you sell," she tells the counterman. "Make that two." She turns to Jake. "I was up all night. How far did I get? Did I tell you about the music lesson?"

Jake wasn't sure on the phone if she was excited or upset. He's still not. There's a hyper, glittery look in her eyes he's never seen before. All he knows is how relieved he is that she's not moving. And how happy she called.

"Y-Y-Y-You said he taught you t-t-t-time s-s-s-signatures in the c-c-c- . . . taxi all night. You s-s-s-said he t-t-t-taught you to s-s-s-sight sing with no m-m-m-music. I-I-I-In the dark."

"Started," she says. "In between picking a guy up at the airport. And driving him to the Bronx. And bringing Dirk in. Oh, man, you have never heard anyone quack like that. And then picking up, like, fifteen other people. We weren't actually in the cab all night. We got home at three thirty. After we got the boys into bed, I just decided it was easier to stay up, so he taught me a few more things on the keyboards, and then we . . ." The counterman brings the coffee to the register. She reaches in her pocket and fishes out three crumpled bills. "Did I tell you Tammy actually had the nerve to ask me for money?" she asks Jake. "Why are you staring at me like that? Is it because I look like a cooked cabbage?"

Jake looks away. "Uh-uh. No."

They walk down the avenue till they get to a stoop. They sit, and while Jake empties many packets of sugar into his coffee, she tells him again about facing down Tammy.

"Did you really th-th-th-think sh-sh-sh-she would take the k-k-k-kids?" he says.

"No," she says. "But I think she wanted to. That could be one of the reasons she won't leave Dad alone."

"Wh-Wh-Wh-What would you have d-d-d-done if she said yes?"

Her eyes darken. "I don't know."

Jake can't get over how brave she is. How even when she was scared, she wasn't tongue-tied. The right words never failed her. She was brilliant. "I don't know how you did it," he says. Which doesn't begin to express it.

"Yeah," she says. "Am I crazy? Am I out of my mind? I mean, here he is, saying we can all go back to Claryville and live like regular, normal people, and I'm saying, No, thanks? Why? I mean, he's saying he wants things to be different, and he wants me to be able to do the things I want to do, but aside from teaching me to sight sing, which he's now saying he wants to do every day, does he have the foggiest idea how? No. He just dreams up some off-the-top-of-his-head-Mr.-Boar's-Head-Baloney salesman scheme. And we know Tammy'll be back. Next time she gets . . . messed up or whatever. And my grandmother's always telling me—"

"C-C-C-C- . . . an I s-s-s-say something?" He has to tell her. Before she gets wound up again. "Wh-Wh-Wh-What you did last night? Th-Th-Th-That . . . was really b-b-b- . . ."

"Yup." She spits the word out.

"D-D-D-Do you e-e-e-even know what I was going to say? I was going to say y-y-y-you were b-b-b- . . . b-b-b- . . . c-c-c-cool," he ends lamely.

"Oh, that's me," she says with a tight nod. "Cool and brave. Do you know how sick I am of being brave!" she says as he folds the sugar papers into smaller and smaller squares. "I would like something to be easy. Just for once I would like something to be a piece of cake. Why do I have to be so cool all the time? Why does everything have to be so hard? I am sick to death of everything in life being hard and messed up and complicated. Why? That's what I want to know."

"The Evil T-T-T-Tongue G-G-G-God?" he says. The demon is clearly on the job today. It feels possible that she's talking about things being hard for him, too. "That's what I used . . . to . . . th-th-th-think," he adds, taking a bigger sip of coffee than he intended, scalding his mouth. "When I was, y-y-y-you know . . . a long time ago."

"So, now we know what was messing up your life," she says. "Who do we blame for mine, the Evil Dad?"

"I like your dad," he says. "I like him a lot."

"Me too!" she shouts. "What do you think makes it so complicated?" And she starts to cry. Not the wracked with sobs, blowing your nose, shoulders shaking, raucous kind of crying. The kind where the tears just suddenly ooze up and roll down your face. It's no less terrible and embarrassing to him, though. It might be worse.

"Sorry," she says, standing up and swiping at her eyes with her hand. "You look like you can't wait to get out of here. I don't blame you."

"Me?" he says. "No. No. I'm okay. You know me. M-M-M-Misery l-l-l-loves company, right?"

"You don't happen to have a tissue, do you?" she says. "I don't know why I did that. I don't cry. I never cry. No. Wait." She digs in her pocket. "I have one. Sorry," she says again as she blows her nose. "I'm fine now."

She's about to start over to the trash can when her face freezes. "Jake!" she says. "It's Eugene! He's about to cross the street! He's gonna see us! Come on!" She grabs his hand and pulls him to his feet. "Jake! Hurry!"

They start to run. They run, still holding hands, all the way to the corner, and then around it. Kira's suddenly laughing. They're both laughing. They run halfway down the block, checking over their shoulders to make sure Eugene's not following, laughing and laughing.

"Whew!" she says when they stop finally. Her face is bright red. Her hand, which was freezing cold, is as warm as his.

"You don't think he saw us?" Jake asks.

"I think we're okay." She's still puffing. "You know how he always looks like he's in his own world?" She makes a serious yet spacey face that looks so much like Eugene that he laughs some more.

"That was a really mean thing we did, right?" she says when they finally stop laughing.

"Uh-huh." He nods.

"He doesn't deserve that."

"No." He tries to make his face look earnest. "No."

"So then . . ." She checks his eyes. "Should we go back?"

The old, crazy, anything-can-happen giddiness rushes over him. "No," he says.

Which makes her laugh again. "You can blame it on me," she says. "You can say I had a meltdown. You can tell him I abducted you." She looks at their sleeves, which are sloshed with coffee, then in her cup. "Guess I didn't want that coffee, huh?"

Jake isn't sure if he should drop her hand now or keep holding it. He keeps holding it. There's a brownstone with a wide stoop a few doors away. They walk over and sit on the second step. It feels somewhat weird to him sitting down still holding hands, so he lets go.

"I wish there was no school today," she says, wrapping her arms around her knees. "I've got a science test second period, and probably a math quiz. I've done no homework. Not to mention: How are we going to explain this to Eugene? I wish I could just go someplace and disappear."

No! he thinks. "Wh-Wh-Wh-Where would you go?"

She shrugs. "I don't know. I saw more of the city last night than the whole rest of the time I've been here. I haven't even been downtown except for last night. Or uptown. Except for the diner, I haven't even seen Flushing. I go to school, I go home, I go to school, I go home. . . ."

"I . . . c-c-c-could . . . sh-sh-sh-show you some places," he says as the giddiness threatens to bubble over. "We could go someplace."

"Like where?" she says.

"Anywhere you want."

"You're the New Yorker," she says.

"We could go to . . ." For some reason, every place he thinks of has *B*s in it: The Bronx Zoo. The Empire State Building. The Brooklyn Bridge. Battery Park. "The St-St-St-Staten Island F-F-F-Ferry," he says finally.

"Want to go now?" she says.

Why not? he wants to say. It's a really nice day. There's enough money on his MetroCard for both of them. He can already see himself side by side with Kira at the railing, eating hot dogs, which he's got enough money for, even if they're expensive, pointing out all the famous New York City landmarks, like the Statue of Liberty and Ellis Island, and whatever, Kira not caring if he stumbles on the names, because she's so happy to be out in the air, looking at the waves in the harbor, eating hot dogs. Because she's so glad to be free. Because she's so happy to be with him.

CHAPTER 27

"I can't," Jake says. "Sorry."

"Right." She's doing that tight, pissed-off nod again. "Hey, I don't go in the subway, anyway. So, don't worry about it. It's cool."

"It's not you," he tells her. "I j-j-j-just . . . swore to myself I wouldn't c-c-c-cut class anymore. I just . . . d-d-d-decided it's . . . not w-w-w-worth it."

She nods again. "Yeah. No. You're right. You don't need more trouble."

"We'll do it, though," he says.

She looks at him. "You promise?"

He picks up her hand again. It's cold. "I promise."

They sit there for a minute looking at their hands with the fingers laced together, Jake's with chewed fingernails, Kira's with the green nail polish. Jake is wondering what to say next when she says, "So, who's this Evil Tongue guy? Is *he* a tongue or is he the god of tongues?"

"The g-g-g-god of tongues," he says. "Not all tongues. Just mine."

He can't believe how dumb that sounds. He waits for her to laugh.

"So, then I guess we can't blame him for Dad's baloney," she says. "And that was his only job? To mess up your mouth?"

"Yes." Even dumber.

"What did he look like?"

Jake's grateful she changed it to past tense; it makes him sound a little less insane. He runs his thumb over her thumbnail. "Green," he says. "And skinny. With dentist tools. A sack of miniature dentist tools. A gunnysack." He planned to stop with "green," but for whatever perverse reason, his mouth is suddenly working perfectly. It's amazing. He keeps going, adding details, making some of it up as he goes along, trying to make it a better story, trying for a laugh, telling her that the Evil Tongue God had long, pincerlike fingers, and tufts of curly hairs growing out of his ears, and nose hairs, and big, black-framed, bug-eye glasses like Ms. Mintzer. She's not laughing. He tells her more anyway, telling her the real stuff now, about how the Evil Tongue God would lie in wait for him in the light fixture, pliers and clamps at the ready, picking his moment; how he could go anywhere Jake went, and usually did; how Jake was always so sure that if he could just psych out the tongue god, make some sense of his rules . . .

"You should have grown up in my house, you know that?" Kira says. "Then when he tried to swing down and clamp you, my grandmother could have whacked him with her fly swatter." She does a vicious backhand swing then slams her hand down. "Whap! Get offa him, you little pip-squeak! Wham! Come near him again, I'll squash you flat!" She snorts. "We should fix him up with Tammy, you know that? They'd probably hit it off great. They could go live in some chandelier in Outer Slobovia. So, what's up with the speech therapy?"

"What?" His heart nearly stops.

"Why don't you go?" Kira asks as if it's a regular, normal, everyday question, like, why don't you go bowling? "It could help you, right?"

"I don't want to." *I sound like I'm six,* he thinks as he hears himself. "My dad's . . . you know . . . went away by itself."

"I didn't know your dad stuttered," she says. "When I called you last night he didn't stutter on the phone."

"That's what I mean," he says.

Her eyes narrow. "How old was he when it went away?"

"I don't know. H-h-h-high school? C-C-C-College, maybe?"

They narrow even more. "You never asked?"

"It . . . uh . . . hasn't come up."

"It's a long wait till college, Jake. You've got a lot to say."

He doesn't look at her. "I'm doing okay."

He wonders if it's time to get to school yet. He checks his watch. It's not. He considers standing up anyway. Or leaving. Though that would mean he has to drop her hand. He thinks about telling her to wipe that lawyer look off her face and give him a break.

"Th-Th-Th-That s-s-s-sounded stupid, didn't it?"

"Yes!" she says. "You think nobody's got anything better to do than think horrible thoughts about you because you stutter? We do. I hate to tell you, Jake. Your stutter is not the number one thing on people's minds. You know what else is stupid? Not trying out for concert choir. It's not like you stutter when you sing! You sing better than almost anyone. I mean, I didn't even know it was *called* sight singing till Dad told me last night, but you can actually *do* it. Well."

"It doesn't matter," he says. "I can't be in it. I'm grounded. T-T-T-Totally."

"For what? Not still for cutting English? That was ages ago. Besides, why would they not let you be in chorus? What sense does that make? You'd think they'd be thrilled that you love to sing."

"We d-d-d-didn't t-t-t-talk about it," he says. *I sound six again,* he thinks.

"You didn't tell them?" She looks up toward the street light and cups her hands around her mouth. "Hello up there! Yo! Evil Tongue God. Swing down and get this guy. He's too dumb to live."

"It's n-n-n-not that easy!"

"Right. So you're just going to weasel out of it? And then you want me to feel sorry for you? No." She drops his hand and folds her arms across her chest. "Forget it. You started this, Jake. You and your duck. You got me into chorus. You made me want to do this. You made me want to sing. There's no one in the whole chorus who likes it more than you. I know. I watch you. It's not like me, where I don't even know if I'm going to end up staying in this stupid city. Not to mention that"—she looks away—"I think Ms. Hill saw me singing in the subway. That's why she wants me to be in the talent show. So if I can't be in it, *I* at least have a good reason why I don't feel bad about it. *You,* on the other hand, have plenty of reasons to feel bad *and* stupid!"

"H-H-H-Hold on," he says. "If we're t-t-t-talking about stupid, that's the stupidest c-c-c-crock of b-b-b- . . . I ever heard! She didn't just ask *you* to be in it, you know. Sh-Sh-Sh-She asked all three of us, remember? And s-s-s-so wh-wh-wh-what if she saw you singing in the s-s-s-subway? That's nothing to b-b-b-be . . . All sh-sh-sh-she cares is that you can sing!"

She looks at him for a minute before she answers.

"Whoa," she says, shaking her head. "This is weird, you know that? You're telling me to get over it. And I'm telling you to get over it. What does that mean?"

"Too Serious for Words"

It means that humming, glowing thing between us is so strong I forget to be tired. I forget my worries. All I can think about is getting to chorus so I can see Jake again. I've had the greatest idea. It came to me two seconds after we left each other, when I walked around one corner to get to school, and he walked around the other. Tomorrow's that early dismissal day. We're done at eleven fifty. Jake and I can go downtown!

I rip through the science quiz. I tear through the math. Mixed in with the excited, good hum, though, is a beetley bad hum. About Eugene. Even if he doesn't have a crush on me, I know I'd go ballistic if my friends ran off on me. I'm hoping Jake's already said something to him. What that would be I have no idea. I just want everything to be cool between us.

It's not. That's clear the minute I see them outside the auditorium. Eugene's doing his twirly thing—never a good sign. Jake looks as tightly wound as Eugene's sleeves. They're not talking.

"Hey." I try hard to keep my voice casual. "How're you doing?"

Eugene shrugs. "Okay."

"Okay," Jake says.

Then why isn't he looking at me? "Yeah?" I ask Eugene.

He pulls his sleeves over his hands again and makes a face.

Jake stays three steps in front of me as we walk into the auditorium, hands jammed in his pockets, as if this morning had never happened.

Maybe it's not between him and Eugene at all. Maybe it's about me.

When we get to our row we go through a whole bumbling "You first," "No, you go ahead," thing about who sits where until I finally say, "Eugene. Sit next to me. You always sit next to me."

Jake's not only not looking at me now, he's giving off strong "Don't talk to me" vibes. *Fine,* I think. *If that's the way he wants it.* He slides in first. Eugene follows. We sit down. Eugene unwraps his lunch. Jake pulls out his lunch. I take out my lunch.

I'm so tired, suddenly, I can hardly chew. This has to be the driest sandwich in the history of the world. I sit there, choking it down, trying to push this morning from my mind, trying to forget that Jake's two feet away from me, until Ms. Hill marches in.

"Okay, now!" she says. "Lunches away. Step up and get your music."

"Argggh!" I hear Eugene mutter as we go up to the stage.

Jake says nothing.

We start off with a piece we began working on last week, a canon. First one part comes in, then the next, then the next. Like "Down by the Station," except it's about angels and heaven, and it's hard. It's also fast. You can't wing it. You have to read the notes, and count like mad, and try not to get flummoxed by the other parts, which would be hard even if Dad had given me ten reading lessons, not just one. Even if I weren't so tired now that I can hardly see.

I sit there and watch the notes go by. Till— "Om*niii*potent!"—Eugene blats it out in the middle of a rest. "Om*niii*potent!" Like a bicycle horn. Or a crow.

Kids snicker. Ms. Hill raps on her music stand.

"She said it was a cannon," Eugene says. "So I fired." He looks hopefully at Jake, so I sneak a look too. Jake's mouth is tight. His eyes look a million miles away.

I check Eugene's part. "You have four measures of rest," I tell him. "See. Four groups of four. I had a music lesson," I add. "From my dad. He's teaching me to count."

"Measure twelve, people!" Ms. Hill says. "And this time, count!"

A minute later, he blares in wrong a second time. "Om*niii*potent!"

"No!" Ms. Hill scolds as everyone but me and Jake bursts out laughing. "No! No! No!" she snaps as he does it yet again. "Measure twelve, everyone! Focus!"

I hardly breathe until the "omnipotent" is safely past. But just as we're getting to the last bar and I'm thinking Eugene is home free, "Gloria!" he sings out after everyone has stopped.

"Nobody laugh!" Ms. Hill warns as he covers his head with his arms and moans. "Eugene, tell me you're not doing this to try my patience. Eugene, what is your problem today?"

He looks so pathetic.

"If it's something I did," I whisper, "I'm really sorry. It wasn't to hurt your feelings."

"Yeah." He gives me a small nod, but doesn't look at me. "Anyway, it's not that."

"It's not?" I sneak another glance at Jake. He

looks like he's trying to bite a hole through his lip. "What's up, then?"

But before Eugene can answer, Ms. Hill has us on our feet for lip trills and head rolls and shoulder shrugs. Then it's on to dynamics exercises. "Let's have something rousing, Ms. Bolden!" she says. "Something to get the blood flowing!"

You wouldn't think you could mess up having your arms down when the piano plays softly and raising them higher as it gets louder. Eugene does. Several times.

"Eugene," Ms. Hill says. Shouts, actually. She's shouting now. "If I didn't have acid reflux before I came in, I do now! If you can't manage up and down how are you going to do your act tomorrow?"

"Argggh!" he moans.

"So I am going to see you all tomorrow for the auditions?" she says when, after more mess-ups and scolding, the rehearsal is finally over. "Alana? Tasha? Felipe? Sonia, darling, I see you trying to sneak out the back door. You'll be there, won't you, Michelle? Eugene?"

We're already headed up the aisle.

"Eugene?"

"Keep walking!" he mutters. Not that Jake needs

any urging. He got out last but he's already headed for the exit.

Ms. Hill catches up with us. "You know, Eugene," she says. "You never told me what your group is planning to do tomorrow."

"Group?" I say as Jake keeps walking. "What group? There's no group."

"Uh . . ." Eugene looks like he wants to sink through the floor.

I suddenly get what's going on—with him, anyway. It's not getting ditched by us. I've been so obsessed with Jake and what he's feeling or not feeling, and what we're doing or not doing, I've totally ignored that Eugene's actually getting up on stage tomorrow.

"Uh . . ." He rattles the Nik Naks in his pocket. "It's . . . not exactly a group."

Ms. Hill looks puzzled. "But you signed up as Dirk and the Dazzlers. . . ."

"He did *what*?" I say.

His face is beyond red now. "Yeah, well . . . you see . . . uh . . . remember, Ms. Hill, when you said that thing to me? About how we can't all be vocal soloists?"

She nods, waiting.

He twists his sleeves up. "I guess I was sort

of looking for a name that didn't sound so, you know . . . solo-like. I know," he tells her. "I know what you're thinking. You're thinking then why'd he—"

"Jake!" Ms. Hill cuts Eugene off.

Jake's been sort of lurking about ten feet up the aisle, not looking at us, but not leaving, either. He jumps, but then he turns around.

She crooks her finger at him. "Jake, come on back over here a second."

I can feel him flinch as she looks into his eyes.

"Surely you and Kira aren't going to make Eugene go out there on that stage alone?" she says. "It looks to me like your friend could use a little support. What are you looking at Kira for?" she adds as—for the first time since this morning—his eyes flick to mine. "Kira may have more experience as a performer . . ."

So I was right when I told Jake she'd heard me in the subway! I knew it! I wait to see what shameful, humiliating, embarrassing thing she's going to say next. She's not even looking at me, though. Her eyes are riveted on Jake.

"I see you back there at every rehearsal," she tells him, "with your nose buried in your part, and each time I ask who wants to take a solo, you just happen to need the bathroom. But you don't fool me for a minute. I've heard how you sing when you think no one's listening. I've seen your face. I can feel you, just like Kira, waiting to shine."

It's exactly what I said to him. The same exact things! And he looks the exact way he did on that stoop—like his body's doing the old, *Danger! Head for the pond!* and his eyes are begging, *More! Tell me more!*

"You've been too serious for too long, Jake," she says. "Too serious for words."

She puts her hand on my shoulder. "Kira, you're standing there nodding your head about Jake, but I'm wise to you, too. You know, it takes one to know one."

One what? I think as the beetles begin swarming again.

Then I see the way she's smiling at me, with that warm, sharp, crazy, powerful smile, and it comes to me. She's not just telling me I'm special this time. Jake was right. She could not care less if I sang in the subway. She's telling me I'm like her.

I almost keel over.

"That's right," she says as the beetles keep zooming. "You and I both know that under all that attitude is a charming, bubbly, and joyous young lady. Let her out, honey! Do us all a favor. Let the girl out!"

"As in tomorrow?" Eugene is practically jumping up and down. "So then you're making them try out with me? You mean I might not have to hide in the supply closet? I don't have to lock myself in my locker . . . oh, thank you, thank you, oh, great and wondrous—"

"Eugene! Shush!" Ms. Hill glares at him.

"And thank you, Jake! I don't care if you and Kira *did* ditch me, if you . . ." His face falls. "Oh, no! I totally forgot. You *can't* be in it. You're gr—" He catches himself. "And Kira can never do anything after—"

"No," I tell Ms. Hill as the beetles hop and skip and fly. "No. I can be there. I'll call my dad right now," I tell Eugene. "We'll rehearse at my place later. And if we pass the tryouts, he'll just have to get a sitter. He said he would. If he can't pay for it, I'll pay for it." *How?* I think. Then I remember. "I still have my return train ticket from when I first came here. I can cash it in, right? Or I'll get a week-end babysitting job. I could do that."

The warmth in Ms. Hill's eyes almost knocks me over again. Until I realize I may have just signed up for a duet with Eugene. I give Jake the most Ms.

Hill-like, most Grandma-like stare I can muster. "That is, I'll do it if Jake does."

Ms. Hill smiles at him. "What do you think, Jake?"

He looks like the Evil Tongue God is about to swoop down and zap him. I don't think he's ever said anything to Ms. Hill before. Not while I was listening. But I'm picking up something else in his eyes too—that same look I saw that first time at my house, when I thought he'd never get his mouth unglued and then he did. I'm also starting to pick up that hum again. Probably not as strong as the one I'm giving off. But it's there. It's definitely there.

Unplugged

"Come in," Ms. Blumberg calls a minute later. "The door's open."

Jake's been planning what to say to Barbara Blumberg ever since he left Kira this morning. It's all he's thought about. He's got the entire conversation worked out, both sides, with answers to a range of possible questions, and substitute words, if needed. The instant his hands touch the doorknob though, he blanks. It's one thing to make up a speech you may or may not deliver at some unknown future date . . .

No. Not "may or may not," he tells himself. *That's Spineless Wimp Boy talking, not Jake Who's Waiting to Shine.* He wipes his hands on his pants and opens the door.

"G-G-G-Good afternoon," he says. "I, uh . . . c-c-c-can't stay. . . ." He's supposed to be at computer science with Eugene. But Ms. Hill kept them so long they were already late, and the thought of listening to Mr. Mooney's dry, droning voice . . .

He carefully doesn't step through the doorway.

"I . . . uh . . . just s-s-s-stopped in for a second. However, maybe . . ."

However maybe what? He can't come back after eighth period. Not when Eugene's already arranged to go to Kira's right after school. Jake already feels like a jerk for avoiding her at chorus. But also, if he doesn't do this now, while those staggering things Ms. Hill said to him are still bouncing in his head, and he can still feel the love in Kira's eyes . . .

He can't believe he just thought that. He stands in the doorway for a second, trying to get his mind around it, wondering if it's true or just wishful thinking, before he notices who's sitting on Ms. Blumberg's sofa, drinking a diet soda and eating a very large chocolate chip cookie.

"Well, look who's here!" Ms. Mintzer cries. "Jake! Hello, stranger."

His brain ices over. His throat knots. Every muscle in his body tenses to run.

But then, suddenly, mixed with the terror is that tingly, buzzy, reckless giddiness again. *It's a test,* he thinks. *I've been tested before. Right here, in fact. And I've passed.* He takes a deep breath in through his nose and explodes it out his mouth. He checks the light fixture.

"Ms. Mintzer," he says.

The joy of hearing her name emerge unmangled gives him courage.

"Would you . . . p-p-p- . . . ?"

He panics again, until he realizes he had no interest in saying please anyway. "C-C-C-Could you l-l-l-leave?" He takes another breath. "I have s-s-s-something to say. N-N-N-Not to you," he adds recklessly. "To . . ." Does he dare chance a *B*? "To . . . . Barbara."

Ms. Mintzer's eyes go wide behind her giant black glasses. "Sure." She sticks her soda in her purse and wraps up her cookie. "Absolutely. No problem." She stands up. "See you tomorrow, Barb."

She's gone. He's passed another test. *So, does that mean I can leave now? Like the last time?* The thought pops up automatically. He eyes the door. He could be out of here in nothing flat.

And then his speech comes back to him, word perfect, exactly as he practiced it.

"Iwasthinkingaboutwhatyousaidaboutchangingmymind." He rushes to get it out before his mind changes again. "I th-th-th-think"—he fights the urge to check the light fixture—"I m-m-m-may have."

Ms. Blumberg smiles at him. "Would you like to try it out and see?"

"No," he says.

She pulls her book out. "How does Monday lunch sound?"

"N-N-N-Not good," he says. Then, with his heart hammering, he adds, "I'll s-s-s-see you then."

He knows he should go to the office for his late pass after that, and then straight to computer science. *No. Not yet.* He races up the back stairs to the pay phone by the auditorium. As he runs, that song of Russell's from the subway starts playing in his head.

> *So get down off that ledge,*
> *Take your butt out that sling,*
> *Tell that girl she's your treasure*
> *And sing one more measure,*
> *Then sing it again and again and again—*
> *'Cause a bad song is better than no song . . .*

He has no idea why that popped up now. It's still playing as he drops his coins in and dials:

> *So stop crying foul, don't throw in the towel . . .*

He has no idea if those are Russell's words or if he's made them up.

"Hello?" his dad says.

"H-H-H-Hey," he says. "D-D-D-Dad? Will you b-b-b-be there when I get home later? I n-n-n-need you to g-g-g-go for a run with me. Dad, I did some things today. I did a . . . b-b-b-bunch of things. Dad, wait till you hear what I did!"

My Turn

Some people can't help getting a little annoying when they're nervous. Some people clam up. One thing I figured out about Kira long ago: Kira gets ferocious.

"Was this a plot, Eugene?" she's yelling. "Were you planning all along on doing a duet with me? Because I don't see Jake here. Did you know he wasn't coming?"

"No!" I swear. "I swear. I talked to him at the end of seventh period. He said—"

"Oh, please. My baloney detectors may not have been working too well lately, but I know baloney when I hear it!"

We're in her living room, after stopping off at the store to replenish my Nik Nak supply and to see if my parents will pick me up here on their way home if it gets late.

"Eugene, take that thing off your head! You are not wearing it in the act. Forget it. We are not doing a comedy routine. Chris, Charlie, don't laugh! You'll

only encourage him! Eugene, would you stop playing with their toys and talk to me? Let's start from
where we are right now. What was your act *going* to
be if Ms. Hill hadn't come along?"

I take off the feather scarf. I stop loading Nik
Naks into the dump truck. I let her rant. Number
one, I don't see Jake here either. He said he'd meet
us once he got things worked out with his mom and
dad, but I've called a bunch of times and no one's
home. Number two, it is getting late. Number three,
she's wrong about its being a plot, but she's right to
be worried. I have no act.

"I have no act," I tell her.

"I knew it!" She flops back on the sofa.

"I was waiting for inspiration to strike."

"And . . . ?" She glares down at me.

I arrange the Nik Nak boxes in a star pattern.
"I'm still waiting." Chris and Charlie are sprawled
out on the floor next to me. "What does the duck say
when he gets on stage and has no act?" I ask them.
"How about . . . I'm a dead duck? I'm a quack?"

"We're all dead ducks!" Kira moans. "And would
you stop with the Nik Naks?"

She gets up and for at least the tenth time goes
over to the window and moves aside the shade. Her
dad's put a padlock on the outside gate in case

Tammy comes back, but Kira's got the shades down anyway. She told me about Tammy's showing up last night. The more I think about it, it's not just the tryouts turning her ferocious.

"Where is he?" she says, peering up the stairs again. "She's never gonna let us off the hook, Ms. Hill. And you want to know the really worst part? Now I *want* to do it."

Just not with me, I think. I can't blame her. When I sing, Wombat runs for the onion bin.

Charlie stops pushing his racing car around and goes over to her. "We can sing the Kira song."

"Yeah, Kiki," Chris says. "That's a good song."

"Yeah, right!" she says. "We could also do 'I Believe I Can Fly.'"

"Maybe your dad has an idea." I'm grasping at straws now. "Maybe Russell can help us. When's he get home?"

"Three thirty," she says.

"In the morning?"

She nods glumly. "Every day."

"So, you, like, make dinner every night?"

"Yup. Speaking of which . . ." She walks over to the fridge and opens the freezer. "Let's see. We can have tacos, tacos, or tacos. I hope you like tacos, Eugene."

I had no idea this was what her life was like. I wonder if Jake knows. "You really don't have any babysitter ever?"

"Not yet."

"We can eat at my house," I find myself saying. "My mom will feed us when they're done at the store. It's fine. She loves feeding people."

"What about Jake?" she says. "What about our act?" She slumps into a chair. "Oh, Eugene, I am so tired!"

I feel like telling her she can take a nap, but I know how well that'll go over.

"Guys!" I say. "Get your jackets. I need to say hi to Dirk."

"Cool!" Chris runs for the closet.

"Get Charlie's too," I tell him. "And while you're at it, put . . ."—I have the strongest, totally unwise urge to call her Kiki—"Kira's scarf back."

"Okay!" He comes to me and gets the scarf.

Charlie pulls on my hand. "Come on, Gene the Bean. Let's play with Dirky the Turkey."

"I'm getting the boats, too," Chris calls.

"And the pail!" Charlie yells to him. He looks up at me. "Can we play duck it in the bucket?"

There's a lot to be said for being the big guy for a change. Who wouldn't like hanging out with people who think everything you say is the best joke they ever heard, even if they don't get it? Who are like, "Your wish is my command"? Who think you're grown-up and excellent? If that happens to be because they're two feet tall, or have webbed feet, well, hey . . . Floating plastic boats and pouring water on Dirk suits me just fine right now.

They're listening so happily to my story of how the Three Ducksketeers saved the duck from certain death they don't seem to notice how dark it's getting, and that it's freezing cold. I'm about to bring them back inside when Kira opens the back door.

"It's Jake!" she shouts. "He's here! He just rang the bell!"

"Jake! Jakey!" the boys cry as we all run through the apartment and up the stairs to the gate to let him in.

"Where were *you*?" Kira yells at him. "It's almost six! I gave up and went to sleep!"

"Yeah, Jake!" I chime in. "We totally gave up on you. We were about to go to my house."

"Careful, children," he says in what I assume is supposed to be Ms. Hill's voice. "I'm in an extremely testy mood today. Do not—I repeat, do not—mess with me. You get me started, you don't know what I'll do!"

He doesn't look testy. He looks like he's eaten Leona's can of catnip.

"Excuse me," Kira says as we follow him down the steps. "We're the testy ones, Jake! We thought you weren't coming! We thought you—"

"Ducked out on us!" I finish for her.

He turns to face us. "*M-M-M-Moi*? J-J-J-Jake 'I'm Not G-G-G-Grounded Anymore' Kandell?"

"For real, Jake? Eugene, did you hear that?" For a minute there, Kira forgets to be ferocious. "See! I told you, Jake! Didn't I tell you?"

Don't hug him, Kira. I beg you.

"Awesome," I say. "So then you're good to go?"

"Uh-huh!" I can't decide if he looks smug or like he's going to erupt. "What are we doing?" He looks at the toys strewn around the living room. "Is the act all ready?"

"Act?" she says. "What act is that? There never was an act. We need an act. Eugene here—"

He smiles. "W-W-W-We may still b-b-b-be okay. Ch-Ch-Ch-Check this out." It's smug. Definitely smug. He does a little air-guitar thing and starts to sing: "Oh, a bad song is better than no song. A bad song beats no song at all. . . ."

"No!" Kira starts waving her arms. "Stop! I hate that song! If I'm getting up in front of everyone and singing a song, it's going to be a song I like."

"It's not R-R-R-Russell's words," he says. "I made them up. J-J-J-Just listen, okay? I mean, d-d-d-do you have another idea?" He sings again: "So stop crying foul, don't throw in the towel. . . ."

I look at her. "That could work. F-o-w-l? What's Dirk doing tomorrow afternoon? We're desperate here, remember?"

Jake sings on:

> *"Take that chip off your shoulder before you*
>   *get older*
> *and your heart gets much colder*
> *and your brain starts to molder,*
> *yeah, try being bolder. Yeah, that's what I*
>   *told her. . . ."*

"No! Forget it! Jake"—she's waving her arms again—"do the words 'over my dead body' mean anything to you?"

"No, think about it," he tells her. "We could, like, t-t-t-take . . . t-t-t-turns, you and me. I sing one line. You sing the next. It's a d-d-d-duet."

"A sucky duet. Not to mention the fact that—"

"I know!" He puts his hands up. "I know. It wasn't just *me* telling *you*. You told me, too. It was j-j-j-just, y-y-y-you know, the only way I could make it rhyme. Plus, it's f-f-f- . . . more amusing this way."

"To you, maybe!"

"Let's try it. There's nothing to lose."

"Your head? My pride?"

"Hey!" I have to shout to get their attention.

"Hey!" Charlie shouts.

"Quiet!" Chris steps between them. "Eugene is talking!"

"So, she gets to shine," I tell Jake, "you get to be less serious, and I get to do what? Play the Nik Naks?"

Boing! goes the proverbial lightbulb.

"Aha!" I shout. "Wow. Whoa. Eureka! Chris! Charlie! Have a seat. Relax. Jake, Kira. Here's what we're gonna do. . . ."

CHAPTER 31

"Gum out, everyone!" Ms. Hill orders. "Take your gum out! This is an audience of your friends, but it *is* an audience, so act professional. Chorus members, please be quiet so your friends can entertain you. Which of you brave souls is going to be our opening act?" Her laser-beam eyes scan the rows. "Fine," she says. "If no one's going to volunteer, I'll do the choosing. How about . . ."

I clasp my hands. "Oh, do not choose us, I beseech you, oh, most merciful Hill goddess . . ."

Ms. Hill chooses a dance group.

Three girls in white leotards and long white skirts slink onto the stage.

"Tell us your names, ladies," she says as if these are three unknown people, three humans she's never set eyes on before. "Tell us what you'll be performing."

One of them mutters something.

"Into the mike, child!" she calls. "We can't hear you!"

"You already know our names," the girl complains.

"*I* know them, but the audience won't," Ms. Hill tells her. "Now hold your head up and give us a proper intro."

I started rewriting my intro during math, but Mr. Moses confiscated it. I remember not one word. I nudge Kira. "When we go on? How about if you announce us?"

She gives me a ferocious glare.

The music starts. One of the girls trips on her skirt. A bunch of kids, including me, snicker.

Ms. Hill leaps to her feet. Her finger shoots out. "You laugh again, I *will* put you out. And then you can forget about being in the show. It happens, honey," she tells the girl on the stage. "Life goes on. We rise above it. Would you like to start over?"

They do. And rise above it. They're excellent.

So are all the acts: a singing duet; a drum group; two rappers; a girl who plays violin about ten thousand times better than I ever did; a girl I've never even seen before, who plays flute, also well; a boy who says, "I know you said last year you didn't want to see any more Michael Jacksons, but . . ."

It's not that I want people to trip, or break a string, or fall off the stage. I'm not sitting here going, "Bomb out. Be bad. Please suck!" I just want them to be less good than us.

"How's your pizzazz level?" I ask Kira. "Mine's fizzled. It's pizzled. I'm frazzled."

She pretends not to hear me.

"And you, my liege?" I ask Jake. "How farest thou?"

Why am I talking like this? This doesn't bode well.

"Beautiful! Whooh! That was just excellent!" Ms. Hill calls to the girl group coming off the stage. "And now let's welcome . . ."—she picks up her program sheet—"Dirk and the Dazzlers!"

"I just want you to know," Kira says as we scramble to our feet. "They laugh me off the stage, you die."

"You?" I say. "What about me?" She and Jake get to wait backstage while I'm out there alone doing the intro.

It's a long hike to the mike. This must be what it feels like to have a wooden leg. My arms dangle like a chimp's.

I'm so glad now I decided not to tell my parents I was doing this.

"Testing, one, two," I say into the microphone.

Unlike rehearsals, where everyone sits in the

first three rows, kids are spread all over the auditorium. They're chatting; they're eating; they've got their feet up on the seats or sticking into the aisles. A girl in the front row is checking her phone messages. This sixth-grader, Marcus, is asleep. Ms. Bolden looks like she can't wait to go home and take some Tylenol.

"Hi," I say into the mike.

Ms. Hill waves back. "Hi, there."

The protein bars Jake's mom gave us this morning, which I ate during third period, mine and his both, have decided they're not happy where they are.

"Would you excuse me?" I say as spots of light dance in front of my eyes.

"Where are you going?" Ms. Hill says.

"I think I might be going to puke," I say.

"Please don't, sweetheart," she says. "I have a weak stomach."

"Pssst. Eugene!" Kira waves her arms at me from backstage.

I stumble over to her. "What are you doing?" I say as she unwraps the feather scarf, reaches inside her shirt, and pulls out a chain.

"It's Grandma's good-luck puke-control charm," she says. "It hasn't let me down yet. Just turn around."

She puts it on me and shoves me back toward the stage.

I step up to the microphone again. "Okay," I say. "I've been telling myself that the good thing about not being cool is that you can't lose your cool."

"True enough," Ms. Hill says.

"Now if I can just not lose my lunch," I add.

She chuckles. I don't know if it's her laugh or Kira's charm; my stomach stops jumping.

"So," I say. "In case you've forgotten. We're Dirk and the Dazzlers. Our group will be featuring . . . me, on, would you believe . . . the Nik Naks." I pull out two Nik Nak six-packs and shake them into the microphone. Ms. Hill laughs. Marcus wakes up. A couple of other kids sit up in their seats. "Also the kazoo." I take it out of my pocket and hum a little *Ta-da!* into it.

It was a close call with the kazoo. First, trying to convince Jake and Kira the kazoo is an actual instrument, it being orange and plastic and left over from second grade. Also, for a while there in English it looked as if Mr. Estrada was going to take it from me. But all eyes are on me now. And they're laughing, but they're laughing the way I wanted them to. I look offstage for Kira. Jake gives me a thumbs-up.

I may be starting to enjoy myself.

"Our group also features . . ."—I hum a short and totally improvised kazoo fanfare—"the inimitably inimitable Jake the Snake Kandell on vocals, and the charismatic and scintillating—"

"Dirk, baby!" Ms. Hill taps her watch. "I hate to interrupt, but we've got umpteen more acts after yours."

"No problem." I signal Jake and Kira to come out. "So, it's the two of them," I tell the audience, "and me, Eugene. Dirk was afraid he wouldn't make it past security. We're performing 'Me and Bobby McGee.'"

I'd love to know exactly what happened after that. I know it started out with Kira singing by herself, fantastically, naturally. And then Jake joined in, singing harmony, also fantastically. And I'm fairly sure I came in with my Nik Nak rattles at the right times and did all the moves we worked out this morning before school, as well as some that came to me then and there. But I'm a little fuzzy about details.

What I do remember crystal clear is playing my kazoo: the way everyone sat up a little straighter that first time I hum-sang the words into the mouthpiece; the cheers and whistles when I did my little bluesy wah-wah harmonica riff on the chorus; the rush I felt when Jake and Kira stepped back from the mike, which was totally unpracticed and unplanned, after the second verse, and let me take a solo. And as I hummed my last na-na-nas and la-la-las, and she sang the last "Hey, hey, hey, Bobby McGee. Yeah!" I remember thinking that this may have been the most fun I've had in my entire life.

And then Jake's clapping me on the back, saying, "Way to go, Dirk, baby!" and Kira's throwing her arms around me so hard she almost knocks me down, and Ms. Hill is shaking her head and shaking our hands, saying, "Now that is a tough act to follow."

"So, are we really going to get up on stage in front of the whole school and do that again?" Kira says as we walk back to her house. Since, needless to say, we passed the tryouts with flying colors. She's trying to look as if that would be just so boring. She's not fooling me. Not with that tackle hug she gave me, and the way her eyes are shining.

"Yes, we are!" I say.

"Yes, we are!" Jake chimes in before I've even finished. "C-C-C-Can I use your phone? I'm . . . th-th-th-thinking about c-c-c-calling my dad." He must *really* be happy. Except for Mintzer, and maybe my umbrella, there's nothing in life he hates more than the telephone. "I did it, Dad," he says. "I d-d-d-did it! And you should have seen Eugene! Eugene was so g-g-g-good! Eugene knocked them out with his kazooing!"

I can feel myself blushing. "Kazooming," I correct him. "I'm a kazoomer. Or possibly a kazoodler."

As soon as he's off, I call the store and tell my mom that I would really like it if they could get someone to fill in for a few hours four weeks from today because I'm going to be kazoodling in a show. Mom's not sure what a kazoo is. She's got customers. But she sounds excited.

"You're c-c-c-calling your d-d-d-dad?" Jake says as Kira takes her cell out too. I didn't know she had a cell. "T-T-T-Tell him how—"

She waves for him to be quiet. "Dottie Stickles, please," she says into it. "Oh, okay. No. She can call me later. If you could just give her a message, though? Tell her, remember how she said I was overdue for something good to happen? Well . . ."— she beams over at us—"tell her it just did!"

She's off the phone and we're halfway to her house when she says, "I am so not ready to go home. It's so nice out today."

"It's like fourteen degrees," I tell her.

"No, it's not. Besides, who cares?" she says. "I want to go somewhere."

"Now?" I say. I've thought of some improvements to my intro. I need to write them down before I forget. There are some kazoo effects I can't wait to try. "Like where?"

She shrugs. "I don't know. Somewhere I've never been. Not Flushing." Before I can say "Huh?" she turns to Jake. "We could go downtown. We could go on the Staten Island Ferry, like you wanted to that other time. Is that a crazy idea?"

Other time? I want to say. *What other time? Why don't I know about this other time?* Instead, I say, "On the subway?" Since, as far as I know, she refuses to set foot down there.

"Uh, yeah." She nods, but not at me. "Yeah!" she tells Jake. "Wanna do it?"

"W-W-W-What about . . . I mean . . ." Jake's not looking at me either. "Doesn't your d-d-d-dad h-h-h-have to go to work?"

"Yes," she says, looking at me finally. "What do you think, Eugene? Would you feel totally bad and left out if Jake and I—"

"Went without me?" *Ditched me again?* I don't say that, or *Yes, I would!* At least she looks totally sheepish and guilty as well as disgustingly happy.

"It's fine," I say after a minute. "Go on downtown, guys. Have a good time."

"You sure?" She looks in my eyes. "Really? You don't mind? And, I mean, I know Tammy can't get in, but what if she calls? And Grandma's gonna call back. You're gonna have to tell her everything. Dad too. He's gonna want to hear every gory detail."

"Not to vorry, cheeldren," I tell them. "I vill handle everything! I vill kahzoodle for zee whole kit and kazoodle!"

I wait for her to make a crack about the Transylvanian accent, which just sort of happened. But looking at her now, you'd never know this girl had ever made a crack in her entire life. For the second time today she throws her arms around me and . . . oh, my God, can this be happening? Kira the Killer is kissing me! "Thanks, Eugene!" she says. "For everything."

For a minute there, I'm afraid Jake might kiss me, too.

"Yeah, Eugene," he says. "You're the . . ." He's stuck. Those killer *B*'s get him every time. He's like me, though. It may take us a while, but once we decide to do something . . . "You're the b-b-b-best!"

CHAPTER 32

It turns out there's not a lot to handle when I get there, and no kazoodling. We must have kept the boys up way too late last night. They're asleep. Tryouts ran so long Russell's worried he'll be late for work and lose his job, so as soon as he makes sure Kira sang well and the rest of us survived, he gives me a few quick instructions and his number, tells me to go ahead and eat anything that looks good, and is out the door.

I'm checking out the fridge, considering calling my mom again, and seeing if things have slowed down enough for me to play for her, when the phone rings.

"So you three knocked 'em dead, eh?" Kira's grandmother says. There's no mistaking who it is. She sounds like an older, scratchy-voiced Kira.

"We were pretty good," I tell her. "Kira was outstanding!"

"And you?"

"Not bad."

"Just not bad?"

"It was actually my kazoo debut. I started out a little nervous, but that good-luck puke-control charm of yours saved the day."

"Puke-control charm?" She snorts, or chuckles. It's hard to know which. "She told you my little diamond horseshoe was a good-luck puke-control charm? That Kira is a piece of work!"

"She made it up?" I sort of knew that, and yet . . . "You're saying she was being nice to me?"

"Well . . ." I hear what sounds like the click of a cigarette lighter. "She said you're pretty nice yourself."

"She did? Wait a minute. You know, this is Eugene, not—"

"I know! She's told me all about you. Jake's the shy singer, and you're the one who keeps everyone entertained. The one my grandsons are so crazy about. Mr. Nik Nak. The one who dreamed up the idea for the act."

"Seriously? She said that?"

"She sure did. She told me last night you're the one who got this whole show going."

I'll sound like a jerk if I say *She did?* again. "I guess that's true."

"And from what I hear, Eugene," she adds, "luck

had nothing to do with it. Any luck you kids have had, you've made yourselves. I'll tell you one thing, though. I'll bet Kira's thanking her lucky stars for meeting you."

I'm thanking my lucky stars there's no one around to see my face!

"So, are you coming down for the show?" I ask her. Since I can't ask if she'd like to be my grandma, too. "Because you know I'd be happy to give you a little kazoo demo now."

She laughs. "That's okay. I'll wait. Eugene, don't you think you should put Kira on?"

"She's not here," I say. "She's out. With Jake."

"With Jake? You mean to say they're off celebrating and you're babysitting the boys?"

"Tell me about it!" It blurts out before I can stop myself.

She takes so long to answer I start to think she's put me on hold. "You're a good friend, Eugene," she says finally. "Giving Kira a chance to get out of that house for a while. If I wasn't a hundred miles away and working, I'd be over there helping her myself."

I suddenly flash on Kira telling me how she'd get a babysitting job to pay for a sitter for the boys. "You know," I find myself saying, "you could give me a few babysitting pointers. Then I could maybe come over and hang out with them a couple of afternoons a week. Yeah. I could do that."

Because Kira really, really wants to be in concert choir. Jake would kill to do it, and now, barring any unforeseen stupidness, he can. And kazoo prodigy or no, I'm not exactly concert-choir material. And even if I must be nuts to help the two of them go off and do something without me, it beats squirting beets.

"How did all this happen?" I ask Dirk after I'm off the phone. The boys still aren't up. I've eaten everything that looked halfway enticing. I don't know how long before Kira and Jake get back, but from the looks on their faces, it won't be soon. I've gone outside.

Dirk's floating in his pool. He lifts his head up when he hears my voice. *"Waaack,"* he says.

"You've got that right!" I reach out and give him a pat.

He doesn't bite me. In fact, he looks delighted to see me. Or as delighted as a duck can look. It's somewhat hard to smile when you have a bill.

"Pretty boring, huh, all alone back here? Round and round, back and forth?"

"Waaack!" he says.

"I know what you mean. Good thing you've got me to entertain you."

I squat down next to the pool. He stretches his neck out for another pat.

"See, you're cheering up already. I don't know why everyone thinks ducks are ludicrous," I say as I stroke his feathers. "You're a handsome devil, you know that?"

"*Waaack*," he says, which I take to mean, "You're not so bad yourself."

"Intelligent, too. A duck of distinction. Speaking of which, how do you feel about the kazoo?"

Whoa! I don't believe it. He's standing up. He's hopping onto the rim of the pool. He's flapping his wings!

"You're in luck!" I tell him. "Feel free to quack along. After that, I've got a few ideas I could run by you. Because, no offense, I think we can come up with a better name for the group."

"*Waaack!*" he says.

"That could work," I say as I wipe the water off my face. "So then I guess it's you and me, Ducko. We'll just hope ducks don't mate for life."

ACKNOWLEDGMENTS

My warmest thanks to Jo Morris, choral director of M. S. 44 in New York City, for letting me listen in. Her musicianship, joy, creativity, and tireless work have inspired and changed countless choir members.

I'm also grateful to Marilyn Atkins, chorus coordinator of M. S. 44, for her generous and enthusiastic help.